CHAPTER 1

"Peter!" his mom yelled from the kitchen. "Are you in your room right now?"

"I'm in the family room!" Peter replied, wondering why his current location in their two-story house mattered so much.

"Then could you please remind me," his mom said, now standing right in front of him with her hands on her hips—indicating she was about to scold him,—"exactly how long you have been in Grade 11?"

Peter's mom was no lawyer, and their family room certainly bore no resemblance to a courtroom, but Peter recognized this technique of *establishing the facts before asking the main question...* (He also knew that a snarky or sarcastic remark would only make his already-irritated mother even more displeased, so he decided to answer her question with fact and nothing more.)

"I just finished my eighth week yesterday," he

replied, not looking up from his disorganized pile of homework on the coffee table.

"I see," his mother said next. "Well, one would think that eight weeks is more than long enough for someone your age to determine that doing homework while watching TV is not ideal, wouldn't you agree?"

"It's just a lab write-up for biology," Peter told her. "And the one I did last month, which I also wrote in this exact same spot, I got 97% on."

"And you are telling me this because...?" his mom commented, urging Peter to continue his side of the argument.

"Cut me some slack," Peter (unwisely) replied. "I'm multi-tasking here."

Peter's mom showed no intention of backing down.

"Multi-tasking... Is that what young adults call *doing homework in front of the TV* these days?" she asked (without wanting to receive a reply.) "I had a feeling you might mention multi-tasking, and I have some bad news for you: I watched a special on it last week. Apparently, people who try to do two or three things at the same time are actually putting a huge strain on themselves."

Peter knew his mom was waiting for him to ask her to expand on that, but he wasn't in the mood to play along.

"In reality," she continued (unprompted), "your

focus is jumping from the TV to your homework, then back to the TV and back to your homework. You're thinking about one thing for a few seconds, then the other, and then back again. And this is WAY more exhausting than just finishing your homework first and watching TV after."

And then she spun around and left the room (like a defense attorney who had just finished her closing argument!)

Peter knew that if he didn't go upstairs to his room soon, his mom would be back for "round two" of this battle: And that was something he didn't feel like doing at all. (Neil was coming to pick him up at five o'clock for a "Saturday night on the town," and he didn't want to be barred from going out.)

He started collecting his horrendous spread of papers, notebooks, and textbooks, which for some reason filled not only the entire surface of the coffee table but had even spilled over onto the floor.

Ring-ring.

"Hello?" Peter said after picking up the receiver.

"Good afternoon," a very professional-sounding voice said. "This is Dr. Reynolds from Stoneburg Memorial. Could I speak to your mother or father, please?"

"Just a minute, please," Peter replied politely, putting his hand over the receiver.

"Mom!" he called. "It's for you!"

* * *

The only phone downstairs was the one in Peter's hand, so his mom walked in, sat down beside him, and accepted the phone from her son.

"Hello?" she said curiously.

Over the next thirty seconds, as she listened intently, her expression changed completely.

"Oh, my goodness," she gasped, putting her hand up to her mouth. "Is he okay?"

CHAPTER 2

"Your brother has been in a car accident," Peter's mom told him when she finished her conversation with the doctor. "I'm going to the hospital to pick him up."

"Is he alright?" Peter asked. (Although the expression on his mom's face indicated she was more "angry" than worried.)

"Dr. Reynolds said Brad's only injuries were a few glass shards in his scalp and a mild concussion," she told Peter. "He was one of the lucky ones. Thomas broke his leg in two places, and Barry has three cracked ribs."

The instant Peter heard his mom say "Thomas," he knew why she was so angry...

* * *

Thomas had been a close friend of Bradley's for ages, but Peter's parents had often wished the two had never met. Thomas was a magnet for trouble: wherever he went, problems soon followed.

During Bradley's first year of college, when he was too busy studying to hang out with Thomas anymore, his parents had thought Bradley's life was finally free of Thomas' bad influence. Bradley had become more serious about his education, plus he had met (and started dating) Bridget.

But everything changed the instant Bradley discovered Bridget was Xavier's daughter, meaning he had been deceived by the only girl he had gone out with for an extended period of time.

Bradley, unfortunately, reverted to his old ways: He was putting a lot less effort into his sophomore year, and his grades were reflecting it. He wasn't going to fail anything, but the shiny 82% average from his freshman year had dropped to 67%.

Not only were his grades slipping, but he was also hanging out with Thomas (and a few of his other old buddies) a lot more regularly.

* * *

"Did someone crash into them?" Peter asked. "Or was the accident Thomas' fault?"

"I'll find out the details when I get to the hospital," his mom replied. "But I do know this much: no other vehicles were involved. Thomas rolled his car, on a county road in the middle of nowhere, while doing almost twice the speed limit."

"I'll come to the hospital with you," Peter told his mom, standing up to put his shoes on.

"You don't need to do that," she answered. "You're getting together with Neil for dinner tonight, right?"

"Yeah," Peter replied. "And then we're gonna play pool or catch a movie."

Peter's mom walked up and stood face-to-face with him. "And you'll be home before ten o'clock?" she asked (ordered?) him.

"Of course," Peter smiled.

"Your father should be back from the driving range soon," she said next. "Tell him where I've gone. Or leave him a note if he's still out when Neil comes to get you."

"Gotcha," Peter replied. "And Mom...?"

"Yes?" she asked back.

"Feel free to scream and yell all you want at Thomas," he advised her. "But don't break his other leg."

CHAPTER 3

Honk! Honk!

The loud noise Neil made by leaning on the horn before pulling into Peter's driveway was completely unnecessary since Peter had been standing just inside the front door—with his shoes and jacket on—the entire time.

"Your chariot has arrived!" Neil announced, driver's window rolled down and arm hanging out.

Peter hopped in, shut the door, and turned down the hideously loud music Neil was blaring on his mom's cheap stereo system.

"Sorry, man," Neil smiled. "I shouldn't have honked. I guess your mom will come out to lecture me in the next ten seconds or so..."

"Not today," Peter replied. "She's at the hospital in Stoneburg: Brad was in a car accident."

"Ouch," Neil said back. "Let me guess...

Thomas?"

"Yup," Peter replied. "Thomas, the doofus, somehow managed to roll his car on a vacant country road."

"How badly was everyone hurt?" Neil asked.

"Brad's pretty much fine," Peter answered. "But a couple of the other guys broke some bones."

"And your mom is going to the hospital to rip Thomas' head off?" Neil asked.

"You sure do know her well," Peter laughed.

* * *

Less than two minutes later, Neil and Peter were on the highway to Stoneburg. The first part of their "night on the town" was going for burgers at Marty's Diner. (It was always a hopping place—meaning filled with teenagers—on weekends.)

While keeping one hand on the steering wheel, Neil tried to look cool and casual as he removed a pack of cigarettes from his pocket and placed one in his mouth. Then he started fishing around for his lighter.

"Very funny," Peter laughed, knowing this was just a joke Neil was playing to see how he would react.

But Neil lit the cigarette, took a big drag, and blew the smoke out the open window. Then he smiled and asked, "You don't mind if I smoke, eh?"

The putrid smell made Peter cough immediately. He quickly opened his own window while saying, "Dude, are you a moron? Put that stupid thing out!"

All sorts of comments were racing through Peter's head: so many that he couldn't pick which one to say first.

Neil took another slow drag of his cigarette (and looked absolutely ridiculous while doing so), proving to Peter that this was not just a silly prank.

Peter moved from the *disbelief* stage to the *unleash some fury* mode. "What you are doing is wrong on so many levels," Peter lectured Neil. "For starters, you're underage. How did you even get those? Did you steal them?"

Peter's comment seemed to rub Neil the wrong way, so he got a bit defensive. "Of course I didn't steal them," he said back sharply. "Charlotte's older sister bought two packs for me."

"Charlotte?" Peter asked. "The Grade 12 chick who lives out in Spruce Valley? Are you still hanging out with her?"

"Occasionally," Neil answered. "Anyway, her sister is twenty-one. I gave her some cash and asked her to buy me some smokes."

"I can't believe I have to ask you this," Peter said next, pausing before making his point. "But, uh... WHY?"

"You don't get it, do you?" Neil said, shaking

his head. "Smoking makes us look older. It'll help us pick up more Grade 12s, or maybe even some college girls."

Peter then began shaking his head as well. (He couldn't believe the gibberish coming out of his best friend's mouth.) "And when did you forget," Peter said next, "that your grandfather died of lung cancer? Which he got from smoking?"

"Dude, he chain-smoked for forty years," Neil replied. "I'm not gonna do that."

"Give me a break," Peter fired back. "Every single smoker starts like that." Then he paused a bit… "And by the way, your mom will smell the smoke in her car tomorrow. She'll ground you."

"The smell won't stick," Neil told Peter. "I'll be safe as long as I keep the window open. Plus, I'm not planning on smoking on the way back."

After Neil chucked the butt out the window (which is both dangerous and illegal!), the drive continued in an awkward silence.

* * *

"Sorry," Neil said a few minutes later. "I won't have any more until we get to Stoneburg."

Once the stench was no longer noticeable (and Peter realized that staying in this negative frame of mind would mean the rest of their night would suck), he decided to temporarily forgive and forget. He twisted the volume knob clockwise and the music from the CD Neil had chosen blared again.

"Oh, I almost forgot," Neil said out of nowhere, quickly turning the music back down. "I made a riddle for you."

Peter smiled and laughed. "Yeah, right," he remarked. "You have never, ever made a riddle."

"I made one, I swear," Neil said back, happy to see both of their moods had improved. "Wanna take a shot at it right now?"

"Definitely," Peter replied, encouraging his friend.

"Oh, and the reason I thought up this one," Neil went on, "was that I was sitting in geography class yesterday, bored out of my skull, when I remembered that you told me thinking up puzzles makes the time go faster."

"And did it?" Peter asked.

"Yeah, the minutes flew by," Neil smiled, reaching into his pocket and handing Peter a piece of paper. "Anyway, we are about seven or eight minutes away from the burger shop. Solve it before we get there, and dinner's on me!"

CHAPTER 4

S *4*   *9* U

N *4*   *9*   *?*

Rule: You only get three guesses!

HI READER! CAN YOU FIGURE OUT NEIL'S FIRST-EVER RIDDLE?

Peter looked up from the paper and smiled. "Am I allowed to write things down?" he asked.

"Be my guest," Neil replied.

Peter didn't have his trusty backpack with him today, but he always carried a small notebook and golf pencil in his pocket.

"And I would get a move on if I were you," Neil remarked. "You've only got about six minutes left."

"I'm holding you to that," Peter commented while pressing the start button on his wristwatch.

Neil gave Peter the "I'll zip my lip" sign, indicating he would stay silent as Peter got cracking on the puzzle.

$$S \quad 4 \quad 9 \quad U$$

$$N \quad 4 \quad 9 \quad ?$$

"Seeing as how the numbers 9 and 4 are in both lines," Peter mumbled to himself. "The answer must have something to do with the letters."

He quickly wrote the alphabet down in his notebook.

A
B
C
D
E
F
G
H
I
J
K
L
M
N

O
P
Q
R
S
T
U
V
W
X
Y
Z

"My first guess is *P,*" he said to Neil shortly after finishing. "And that guess is based on the relative locations of the letters in the alphabet. In the top line of the riddle, there is an *S* and *U,* right? Well, *U* comes two letters after *S* in the alphabet. So in the second line, two letters after *N* would be *P.*"

"Strike one," Neil giggled, keeping his eyes on the highway.

Since Peter was kind of expecting his first guess to be wrong, he wasn't the least bit surprised. (The only reason he decided to use one of his three guesses here was just in case Neil had tried to fool him by making the solution ridiculously simple.)

Neil could see Peter thinking a mile a minute, and couldn't resist making a sarcastic comment.

"I'm sure glad I spent twenty minutes of geography class thinking this puzzle up," he chuckled. "Watching you rack your brain like this is totally worth it."

Peter's eyes stay focused on his notes.

"I'll tack on an extra minute," Neil told Peter. "Since I was supposed to stay quiet the whole time."

* * *

Peter's stopwatch had just passed 4 minutes, so there were only two minutes remaining before reaching 6. After adding the extra one Neil had just offered, that meant he had a total of 3 minutes left.

"Wait a second," Peter said, suddenly perking up.

$$S \quad 4 \quad 9 \quad U$$

$$N \quad 4 \quad 9 \quad ?$$

"I think I see what you were doing," he continued. "The numbers in the riddle are meaningless. You were simply spelling a 4-letter word: *S U N something...* Or if I go down instead of across, *S N U something.*"

Neil didn't respond, as he knew Peter's comment was probably a way of probing for a hint.

"If I start with *S U N,*" Peter said right after

that, "there are three possibilities: sung, sunk, and suns."

Neil smirked, but kept quiet.

"Darn, maybe I doomed myself by wasting one guess," Peter went on. "Hold on, what if I use *S N U something...?*" He paused while running his eyes along all 26 letters of the alphabet. "Well, for that order, I've got two options: snub, or snug."

Neil was now whistling, hoping the sound from his lips would block his ears from hearing Peter's rambling. (He didn't want his reaction to become a tip.)

"Wait," Peter then smiled. "*G* works for both. *S N U G* - snug, and *S U N G* - sung. It's *G!*"

"Are you still speaking to yourself?" Neil asked, wanting clarification. "Or is that officially a guess?"

"*G!*" Peter said again loudly. "I'm right, right?"

"Strike two, dude," Neil laughed. "And although I can't see your watch, I would think you probably don't have much time left."

Peter, unfazed by the lack of time remaining, kept cranking through ideas.

"I think I'll spend most of my future geography classes concocting riddles for you," Neil commented. "This is an awesome form of entertainment."

Peter froze... Then he turned to Neil and smiled. "I can't believe I didn't pick up on your hints," he laughed.

"Hints?" Neil replied, laughing as well.

"You have now used the word *'geography'* three times while I have been doing this riddle," Peter commented. "That was not accidental."

"Hmm..." Neil smiled, trying not to agree or disagree.

$$S \quad 4 \quad 9 \quad U$$

$$N \quad 4 \quad 9 \quad ?$$

"Geography..." Peter continued. "The study of the Earth. Or maybe I could say the study of the *globe?* The *S* and *N* are referring to south and north. And the *4* and *9,* when put together, become 49, which is referring to the 49th parallel."

"Almost out of time, man," Neil said, egging his friend on. "It's now or never."

"What's south of the 49th parallel?" Peter went on. "The United States of America! So there's your *U* from the first line of the riddle. And north of the 49th parallel is...?" Peter smiled. "Of course, Canada! The answer is *C! C* for Canada!"

"Good thing I brought an extra twenty bucks," Neil laughed, giving Peter a high-five. "Just don't order the most expensive burger on the menu, eh?"

CHAPTER 5

"Yes, Mr. um... Smith," the front desk clerk at the ritzy Stoneburg Royal Hotel said to Vasilios. "Banquet Hall C is set up for your group this evening."

"Wonderful," Vasilios said back. "And just to reconfirm: We get the hall from six to ten p.m. Plus, once the dinner clean-up is finished at about half past seven, we are to be left in private until we vacate the room."

"Precisely," the polite guest service employee smiled. "All hall staff have been briefed on those details. And as we discussed the day before yesterday, the fee for the room and buffet dinner is $3,450."

"Here's four thousand," Vasilios replied, placing forty crisp one-hundred-dollar bills on the counter. "Please split the tip amongst your staff."

"How very kind of you, sir," she replied while quickly counting the bills. "Your generosity is much appreciated."

Vasilios then turned to head back up to his room, as there was still over an hour to go before dinner.

* * *

When Vasilios's entire colony (all 130 of them) had arrived on Earth after fleeing Chronostil, they had, of course, needed some place to stay. Since Clearville only had one small hotel, the only option was to take everyone to Stoneburg and put them up in the Stoneburg Royal.

The staff didn't know what to think when one hundred and thirty cloak-wearing individuals suddenly entered their front doors. But since it was the off-season—meaning they easily had enough vacant rooms to accommodate everyone—they happily let them stay. Not only that, but when Vasilios said he would pay in advance for all of their rooms (for a full month) the owner smiled from ear to ear.

Peter knew the hotel staff would be overly suspicious—possibly even enough to warrant a phone call to the police—so he gave Vasilios a "sort-of-realistic" story to use: He was to tell the staff that they were a conglomerate of stockbrokers, and that all their children were being home-schooled. They had come to Stoneburg to plan out investment strategies, far away from the nosy ears of their competitors. And the cloaks were simply a way to make themselves appear a little less professional (and have a bit of fun.) Peter forgot to think up a fake name for Vasilios to use, so when filling out the forms while checking in, Vasilios put the first name that popped into his head: Matthew Smith.

And to help make their tale a little more believable, Peter had quickly set up subscriptions to the four biggest financial newspapers in the country. Every morning, four big stacks were dropped off at the hotel before dawn. The staff happily assisted by putting one of each outside everyone's room before 6:00 a.m.

* * *

"Leonardo," Vasilios said into his hotel room's phone at a little past five o'clock. "Everything is set. They've given us the biggest banquet hall for tonight."

"Excellent," Mr. Winchester replied. "I can't wait."

"It's too bad that Peter and his friends aren't joining us," Vasilios said back. "Those kids have grown on me."

"Well," Mr. Winchester explained. "They are teenagers. And it is the weekend."

"True," Vasilios agreed.

"But don't fret," Mr. Winchester said before hanging up. "Peter dropped off the instructions for a challenge he came up with: One that only I have been told the solution to."

"Fantastic," Vasilios replied. "The last one he made was spectacularly difficult. Is this one as hard?"

"You'll have to judge that for yourself," Mr. Winchester laughed. "See you at six."

CHAPTER 6

"Got the digits," Neil told Peter after returning to their table at Marty's Diner.

By "digits," Neil was referring to the phone number of one of the waitresses. She wasn't waiting on their table, but when Neil saw her wink at him—or at least that's how he had interpreted it—he went over and chatted with her for a few minutes.

"You're on fire, man," Peter commented. "You pick up girls left, right, and center."

"It's all about the aura you put out," Neil smiled. "Chicks dig guys who exude confidence."

Peter almost coughed up his soft drink after hearing that comment. "Do you go on dates with all of them?" he asked.

"Some, not all," Neil replied. "But the more options, the better."

Although Peter thought Neil's approach to dating was not ideal, he didn't feel like debating the matter.

"Check out those two," Neil said, pointing at two high school girls sitting three tables down from them.

"Isn't one phone number from here enough?" Peter asked.

"You must be joking," Neil replied. "Now c'mon, you go and talk to those two. I'll hold down the fort."

"Me?" Peter asked back. "Why?"

"'Cause if the waitress sees me chatting them up," Neil answered, "then she'll think I'm a jerk."

CHAPTER 7

The buffet prepared by the skilled culinary team at the Stoneburg Royal was nothing short of dreamy. Their gathering of 139 (Vasilios' full crew and the residents of Mr. Winchester's home) ate, chatted, laughed, and then ate some more.

The only person who had to miss out on tonight's festivities was Demetrius, as he had been feeling under the weather for the past few days. His fever had thankfully gone down, but he was still stuffed up and coughing occasionally. Sapphire had offered to stay home with him (so he wouldn't have to be alone while everyone else was having fun) but he told her that that wasn't necessary.

* * *

When everyone at the massive gathering was stuffed to the gills, and the tables had been completely cleared of dishes, the head caterer closed the big banquet hall doors and gave a polite nod to Vasilios.

"We have the room for about another two hours," Vasilios announced to everyone. "Shall we talk business first and play afterward? Or vice-versa?"

"We wanna try Peter's challenge now!" Orion—Vasilios' 11-year-old grandson—yelled.

"Anyone disagree with Orion's suggestion?" Vasilios queried the attendees.

Orion then started chanting, "Challenge! Challenge! Challenge!"

In no time at all, the entire room joined in on the chant. (Looks like business matters had been postponed until later...)

* * *

Zoltan and Torin unpacked the supplies that Peter had written down as being necessary for the challenge, and they quickly began setting everything up. Today's challenge was a relay of sorts, so they needed to set up a row of five pylons. (Four orange ones to mark the places where each member of the 4-person team was to stand. And the fifth one—which was green—to indicate the finish line.)

There was a three-and-a-half-meter gap between each pylon. (They used a tape measure to make sure it was the exact length.) Therefore, the total distance that had to be covered by a team was fourteen meters. (Good thing the room was big!) The bag of supplies also contained a stopwatch, four stainless steel tablespoons, and a dozen hard-boiled eggs.

"Any volunteers to go first?" Mr. Winchester asked loudly, even before he had read the instructions to everyone.

About fifty hands shot up.

"Let the children be the first ones to try," Sapphire suggested.

Vasilios knew the names and ages of everyone in his group, so he quickly called up the four youngest kids whose hands were in the air.

Mr. Winchester then unfolded the instructions to the challenge.

An "egg"-cellent race, ha ha!

Task:

Each person on your 4-member team is to stand by an orange pylon. And each person is to hold a spoon in his or her mouth.

An egg will be placed on the spoon of Person 1.

Person 1 must then walk (or run) to Person 2, and transfer the egg to Person 2's spoon.

Then Person 2 does the same to get the egg to Person 3, who then repeats the same thing to get it to Person 4, who finally walks across the finish line.

Rules:

To complete this challenge, you must do it in under 60 seconds.

All four members must hold their spoons in their mouths the entire time.

And this goes without saying, but (of course) you can't use your hands to hold the egg in place while walking, as that would make this game far too easy!

Finally, if the egg falls, that attempt is voided.

The four selected kids (Orion and three 12-year-old girls) needed to decide their order before beginning. Two of the girls said they didn't have any preference, but one girl and Orion both wanted to go last, (to be the one to victoriously cross the finish line, perhaps?)

Orion and that girl faced each other, and both put their right hand in front of them. They were going to decide by using a game called "waterfall-fire-wood," which was basically the weather god version of rock-paper-scissors. (Waterfall puts out fire. Fire burns wood. Wood blocks the waterfall.)

The girl showed "waterfall" and Orion showed "fire," meaning she had won the right to be fourth.

"Can I be first, then?" Orion asked his team.

* * *

As soon as the four kids were in position, each with a spoon in his or her mouth, Zoltan (who had a hard-boiled egg in his right hand and the stopwatch in his left) got ready to place the egg on Orion's spoon.

"I'm putting it on now," Zoltan said to him. "But don't start walking until I say, 'Go.'"

"Okay, I'm ready anytime," Orion tried to say. (But he was holding a spoon in his mouth, so his comment sounded a bit jumbled.)

"Go!" Zoltan said as he pressed the start button.

Since most kids have a good sense of balance (and are light on their feet), Orion quickly and easily got to the next girl. But now came the hard part: getting the egg from his spoon onto her spoon without dropping it.

The girl was quite a bit taller than Orion, so she had to squat a little in order for their spoons to be level.

As the crowd watched intently, Orion slowly tilted his head to the right. The girl's spoon was in the perfect position, and the egg slid onto her spoon, much more easily than they had expected.

The girl then cautiously turned and made her way to the next girl, who was waiting by pylon number three.

This exchange was wobblier than the first one, but thankfully the egg didn't fall. The girl who had just received the egg then began turning around to head toward their team's anchor.

But on her third step, Zoltan announced, "Time!"

"Already?" she said, surprised. "We were barely even half done."

"Give them a second shot!" one of Vasilios' elderly friends yelled.

"Excellent idea!" another agreed.

* * *

The group's second try was a little better than their first, but they ran out of time during the final transfer.

"This is hard!" the third racer on their team—the girl who had been in possession of the egg both times when the 60 seconds had elapsed—said.

"Sure is," Orion agreed.

* * *

Twenty minutes (and six teams) later, the challenge had yet to be successfully completed.

One group had actually managed to get the egg to their team's anchor, but time had run out right after that. And the other five groups had dropped the egg when trying to move too quickly.

Mr. Winchester, who had been sitting on a chair by the finish line, was giggling away the whole time.

Orion noticed the old man's giggling, and that got him thinking… *("If I carefully watch his reactions, maybe he'll provide me with a hint…")* "Zoltan, could you read us the rules again?" he asked loudly.

"Of course," Zoltan replied.

Rules:

To complete this challenge, you must do it in under 60 seconds.

All four members must hold their spoons in their mouths the entire time.

And this goes without saying, but (of course) you can't use your hands to hold the egg in place while walking, as that would make this game far too easy!

Finally, if the egg falls, that attempt is voided.

Although everyone had been listening to Zoltan's voice, only Orion had been *really listening.* He had also been looking at Mr. Winchester the entire time, to see if the old man's expression might provide a hint... And it did!

Orion quickly huddled with his team members and whispered something to them. Then he raised his hand and asked, "If no one else is set to go next, can we have a third try?"

Mr. Winchester, who loves to see youngsters in problem-solving mode, replied, "Certainly!"

The four kids, who all had big smiles on their innocent faces, got into position.

"Go!" Zoltan announced when the egg was on Orion's spoon.

Orion moved (at more or less the same speed as his previous attempts) to the second pylon. When he got there, he stopped... But then he used his hand to take the egg off his spoon and place it on the girl's spoon!

The crowd roared with laughter. (These kids weren't trying to complete the challenge; They were just having fun!)

The rest of their team completed the transfers in a similar manner: using their hands to move the egg from one person's spoon to the next.

When the fourth girl crossed the finish time before time had elapsed, all four kids (and the on-looking audience) applauded and cheered.

When the room quieted down, Zoltan smiled

and said, "Well, if you hadn't cheated with those transfers, then you would have been victorious."

"They didn't cheat," Mr. Winchester said loudly. Then he stood up and congratulated the victorious foursome. "Orion, please explain."

"The trick was hidden within the rules," Orion announced. "It said we couldn't use our hands to hold the egg *WHILE WALKING,* but it didn't say we couldn't use our hands while standing in one spot to transfer the egg to the next person's spoon."

"Argh!" one of the teenagers laughed. "That Peter fooled us all!"

"Again!" another added.

* * *

Zoltan then announced it was time to begin the meeting. Everyone aged sixteen and older was to sit down at one of the tables. The younger ones could do as they pleased, as long as they remained relatively quiet.

* * *

When everyone was seated, Zoltan went to the front to begin his update.

Knock-knock.

All 139 heads craned to look over at the door.

Knock-knock.

This time, the door opened a little, and the head caterer put his face in.

"I'm terribly sorry to interrupt," he said apologetically. "But one of your guests has just arrived."

Sapphire rolled her eyes... "I can't believe Demetrius couldn't sit still and stay home," she said, shaking her head.

"I guess curiosity got the better of Dad," Zoltan added.

The staff then held the door open for the latecomer.

But it wasn't Demetrius!

"Argon!?" Zoltan said in shock. "What!? How...? Why...?"

CHAPTER 8

"Dude," Neil said to Peter as they got back in his car after dinner. "Let's cruise Fairfax Street for a while before hitting the pool hall."

* * *

Fairfax Street was the "hip place" in Stoneburg: the area where high school kids congregated on Friday and Saturday nights. (Neil obviously wanted to see if he could add to his already long list of girl's numbers...)

* * *

"Pretty dead tonight, eh?" Neil said as they started their third pass of the street. "The only chicks I've seen so far were already talking to guys."

"Let's go play pool then," Peter suggested, getting a tad bit impatient. Then he added a sarcastic comment. "Perhaps your dream girl is waiting for you there??"

When they approached the final intersection of Fairfax Street and stopped at the traffic lights, two girls started crossing at the crosswalk.

Neil had kept his window open for their entire "cruise," so when the girls were close to his car, he said, "Evening ladies. My friend and I are heading to play some pool, wanna join us?"

One of the girls appeared impressed by Neil's boldness (and good looks), so she barely even hesitated.

"You should know we aren't supposed to hop into cars with strangers," her friend said to them.

Neil noticed that both girls were now hesitating, so he acted quickly. "Here's my driver's license," he said, passing it out the window to them. "You can hold onto it while we drive there."

"Neil Bannister," one girl said while looking at it.

"The one and only," Neil smiled. "So what do you think? You ladies up for some pool?"

The girls whispered something to each other and once they had decided this *Neil Bannister character* was not a threat—plus the undisputed fact that they had come to Fairfax Street to meet guys in the first place—they opened the car doors and hopped in.

"I'm Emily," the slightly taller of the two said.

"And I'm Heather," the other added.

And then Peter watched (in disgust) as Neil lit up his second cigarette of the day. "Care for a smoke, ladies?" he asked them.

Peter shook his head. (An underage kid was now offering cigarettes to other underage kids... When did Neil lose his morals?)

"Yeah, sure," Emily replied.

"Me too," Heather said next.

The stench in the car was appalling. Peter's irritation was driving his anxiety higher and higher, and he could feel his heart pumping way faster than usual. He just wanted to arrive at the pool hall—which he knew was a non-smoking establishment—to save his nose and lungs from this wretched punishment...

* * *

The girls (who turned out to be in Grade 12) were both quite friendly and funny. No one in their group could play billiards well at all, so it was casual and silly entertainment.

Peter—who was getting a bit better at reading girls' intentions—had figured out the obvious: both girls liked Neil, and neither were interested in him. (But since this had happened before, it didn't bother him that much today.)

* * *

"I'm going outside for a smoke," Neil said about twenty minutes after they started playing. "Anyone wanna join me?"

Both girls grabbed their jackets immediately.

Peter was now standing alone at the pool table... Since they were paying for the use of the facilities, he decided to practice some bank shots until they returned. (I mean, what else could he do?)

* * *

Roughly six minutes later, the three returned (all smelling putrid now) and they started a new game.

* * *

When that game finished, the two girls came up to Neil, and Heather asked him, "Can you score us some smokes?"

"Sure," Neil answered, handing them the cigarettes and lighter. "But hey, I think I'll join you."

Now Peter was alone again!

He didn't feel like playing "solitary pool" again, so he sat down on one of the chairs near their table.

* * *

Exactly eight minutes later, he was still sitting by himself...

"How long does it take to smoke a cigarette?" he asked himself, looking down at his watch for the fourth time.

* * *

When their smoke break crossed the 10-minute mark, Peter had had enough.

"This is insane," he complained.

He walked up to the front desk and asked how much the hourly fee was.

While counting through bills and small change

to pay exactly half of that fee, he returned to their table, placed his money on the felt beside the cue ball, put his jacket on, and stormed out the front door.

Neil and the two girls were, of course, still standing by the corner of the building, smoking away.

"Petey," Neil said, waving him over. "Come out to join us?"

Without making eye contact, Peter kept walking. "I didn't come here to sit at a pool table by myself while you three give yourselves lung cancer," he said angrily. "I'm going home."

"We were about to head back inside a few minutes ago," Emily said, "but then we decided to have a second butt."

"And how are you planning on getting home?" Neil asked. "I drove us here."

Peter stopped, turned around, and stared at them. "If you are concerned about the cost of the table rental," he said sharply. "I left more than enough to cover my share by the cue ball. And Neil, I'll find my own way home."

As Peter was turning to walk away, he heard one of the girls say, "Why is your friend so lame?"

He ignored that remark and kept walking. But then he heard someone, presumably Neil, jogging to catch up.

"Look, man," Neil said. "I'm sorry. C'mon on, come back in, we won't smoke—"

"Neil!" Peter said loudly, turning around to face him again. "I'm sick of being your wingman. You only drag me out because it's harder to pick up girls by yourself, right?"

"Pete, there aren't any buses from here to Clearville," Neil said, stating the obvious. "How are you gonna get home?"

"You worry about you," Peter replied. "And I'll worry about me."

Neil was now frustrated because Peter's behavior was going to ruin his chances with these girls. "Suit yourself," he barked back.

Peter, shaking his head, started down the sidewalk.

(But, um... how was he going to get home?)

CHAPTER 9

"I suppose hitch-hiking back to Clearville is not my best option," Peter mumbled while walking pointlessly around the unfamiliar Stoneburg downtown core.

In reality, he only had two options to resolve his current predicament. One: go back to Neil and apologize—something that he absolutely would NOT do—or two: call home and ask his mom, dad, or brother to come and get him.

"I hope Dad or Brad is home," Peter commented to himself. "Mom would grill me with questions the whole way back about what Neil and I are arguing about."

* * *

A few minutes later, Peter spotted a couple of pay phones about a block away. They were adjacent to what looked like a bus stop, one likely used by a large number of commuters during the work week. But since it was currently a little past eight o'clock in the evening (on a Saturday), there were only a few people waiting tonight: a happy-looking young couple standing hand-in-hand, and a middle-aged woman sitting on a bench, reading. While heading toward the pay phones, Peter dug through his pocket for a quarter.

He picked up the receiver, popped his quarter in the slot, and started punching his home number in.

As he was about to enter the second-last digit, a hand (out of nowhere!) suddenly pushed the lever for the phone down. Peter heard the noise indicting his quarter had come back out.

"Sorry to startle you, Peter," a voice said.

Zoltan!?

"How did you know I was stuck in Stoneburg?" Peter asked, almost stumbling because of how surprised he was. "You guys spying on me?"

Zoltan giggled. "You are the last person in the world we would feel the necessity to watch over," he laughed.

"Then how did you know where I was?" Peter asked back curiously.

Zoltan pointed to Peter's wristwatch. "Did you forget that we installed a tracking device in that?" he smiled.

"Oh, right," Peter admitted. "But that still doesn't explain..." He paused. "Anyway, what is so important that you are chasing me down at this time of night?"

"Peter," Zoltan whispered, looking back and forth to make sure no one was listening in on them. "Something very serious is going on, and we need you to hear it first-hand. C'mon, everyone is waiting for us."

Peter smiled. "I get it," he laughed. "You are planning on surprising everyone at the party by having me crash it unexpectedly, right?"

"I only wish it were for a fun thing like that," Zoltan said with a flat expression on his face. "Alright, let's go. We have to find a secluded place where I can make a twister to get us out of here without being seen."

CHAPTER 10

As Zoltan's tornado zipped them to the Stoneburg Royal (which was less than a couple kilometers away), Peter's mind was filled with questions about why they "needed" him this evening. (The only relieving thing was he would learn the answers very soon...)

When they were about five hundred meters from the hotel, Zoltan lost concentration (or dozed off?) for a few seconds, and the tornado rapidly began slowing down.

"Zoltan, what's going on!?" Peter yelled.

"I have no idea!" Zoltan replied in a panic. "This has never—"

Whoosh!

They were now accelerating toward Earth at approximately 9.8 meters per second. (And since they weren't that high up, that meant it wouldn't be long before they would slam into the ground to their deaths!)

Zoltan focused as hard as he could, and the tornado reformed. But within a few seconds, it became an enormous one, whipping them around at terrifying speeds.

"Slow it down!" Peter screamed. "I feel like I'm gonna pass out!"

Zoltan, baffled by how his typically accurate skills were suddenly so haphazard, tried to weaken the tornado, but couldn't.

"Hold on!" he shouted at Peter. "I'm gonna try to blast us out of this thing!"

He conjured up an upward gust of wind, which blasted them out the top of the terrifying twister. Once out, he created a new and smaller tornado, which this time seemed to maintain its proper size.

Heart racing, Zoltan guided them safely to the roof of the hotel parking garage.

"Zoltan, look at your pocket," Peter said.

Zoltan looked down to see what appeared to be a pulsating green light. He put his hand in his pocket, removed the amulet, and they both looked at it in wonder.

"Has it ever shone on and off like this before?" Peter asked.

"No, never," Zoltan replied.

Over the next twenty seconds, the pulsating gradually became dimmer and dimmer, until it stopped.

"That was weird," Peter said. "It's like the amulet has a mind of its own."

CHAPTER 11

"Peter, this is Argon," Zoltan said once they were in the banquet hall. "He is one of the ten current lead weather gods."

"It's a pleasure to meet you, sir," Peter said nervously while shaking this very important individual's hand.

The majority of Vasilios' colony had already gone up to their rooms. (Only his five most trusted friends remained, as they would likely have some useful input to the upcoming discussion.) Add the current residents of Mr. Winchester's house (except for Demetrius, of course) plus Peter and Argon: and that made for a total of seventeen at this meeting.

"Peter, as I very briefly explained to everyone right after arriving," Argon began, "I have come because of a dire situation back on Sevlar."

"Dire?" Peter asked. "Is Xavier's army growing even faster than we expected?"

"Possibly," Argon replied. "But that's not why I

am here."

"Peter," Mr. Winchester said, trying to speak calmly. "Xavier's men broke into the lead weather gods' meeting room and kidnapped them."

"Kidnapped?" Peter said, panicking a little. "How? When? And where did they take them?"

"We asked Argon to hold off telling us the specifics until you arrived," Mr. Winchester said. "Argon, we are all ears now."

"Unfortunately," Argon said while shaking his head sadly. "He has taken them to Dendaxtra."

The only other person in the room who had ever heard the word "Dendaxtra" was Zoltan. (And the only reason he knew of it was that he had overheard it being mentioned when he was sneaking around the lead weather gods' meeting room as a kid.) But he had no clue what or where it was referring to.

"I'm afraid none of us are familiar with that place," Mr. Winchester told Argon.

"Oops," Argon commented. "I guess I forgot about that. All references to Dendaxtra were omitted from Sevlar's documents close to three hundred years ago. The fact that Dendaxtra even existed is one of the most embarrassing things about Sevlarian history. I only know about Dendaxtra because each new lead weather god is told that information when they begin their tenure; But writing anything down about it is strictly prohibited."

"Another one of your group's stupid, archaic rules," Sapphire said sharply. "No wonder poor Demetrius was so stressed as a lead weather god."

"Your husband pushed hard for us to reinsert the details of Dendaxtra into history books," Argon told her. "As he believed the teaching of past mistakes would prevent something similar from happening again."

"But none of your predecessors' thick skulls agreed with him, right?" Sapphire asked accusingly.

"Unfortunately, no," Argon replied softly.

"Well, spare no details now," Torin told Argon. "The more we know, the better."

"Before The Weather God Academy was built," Argon went on, "which has been in use for the past three hundred years now, Dendaxtra was used as a way to determine whether or not someone wanting to become a weather god was talented and intelligent enough."

"Like some kind of test?" Cynthia asked.

"Yes, I suppose that would sum up its overall purpose," Argon replied. "It was a series of challenges, that had been built inside a mountain, at a secret location."

"What's the big embarrassment?" Mr. Winchester asked.

"Unlike the entrance test for the current training academy," Argon said next, "this one was, uh... a little dangerous."

"Dangerous?" Gabriella asked. "You mean some of those who did the tests were occasionally hurt?"

Argon looked down. "Not occasionally," he replied sadly. "Regularly... Quite a lot were badly injured, and some even died."

"Died!?" Sapphire yelled. "Our ancestors allowed young Sevlarians to die? Just because they wanted to earn the right to become weather gods?"

"Now you can see why this part of our history is something we wish had never happened," Argon replied uncomfortably.

"This is a lot to process," Peter admitted. "But I have a few questions: Not about the past, about now. You managed to avoid being kidnapped, so they must still be looking for you."

"When they raided our meeting room," Argon explained, "intending to kidnap all ten lead weather gods, I hid behind a tapestry."

"So they only caught nine?" Torin questioned.

"Quite the contrary," Argon told everyone. "There were eleven of us in the chamber. Augustus will be retiring soon, so Ignatius, who is set to take Augustus' post later this year, has been joining our meetings to familiarize himself with how matters are conducted."

"They simply took the ten they saw," Mr. Winchester commented. "Assuming all ten were leaders."

"Precisely," Argon answered.

"But they must have noticed your ship departing from Sevlar shortly after this happened?" Torin asked next.

"I never could have used my own ship," Argon explained. "I snuck onto a food supply vessel. I told them who I was, and ordered them to bring me here."

"And where are *they* now?" Gabriella asked. "The crew of the supply vessel?"

"At Leonardo's house with Demetrius," Argon answered. "When we landed near Leonardo's home, Demetrius instructed me how to find everyone here at the hotel."

"Mr. Winchester, we should go back to your house to finish this discussion," Peter suggested. "Demetrius used to be a lead weather god. He could definitely help us out."

"Agreed," Mr. Winchester nodded. "Shall we go via taxis?" Then he smiled... "Or save some money and go by *air?*"

CHAPTER 12

Mr. Winchester's living room now had so many people in it that it almost looked like a fraternity party. About half of them were sitting cross-legged on the floor, a few were using the bottom bunk beds as "sofas," and others were standing by the walls or windows.

"What I fail to understand here," Demetrius commented after being filled in on all the details, "is what their motive was behind this kidnapping. Technically, no one on Sevlar even knows the weather gods were kidnapped, right?" He looked down for a few seconds and began shaking his head. "Wait, I think I may have a guess as to what is going on... The weather gods conduct all their meetings in private, and make all public announcements remotely. We know Xavier has the latest computer technology and some of the best engineers on Sevlar; He's going to make and broadcast fake videos, using the meeting room's broadcast system."

"And since those will show up on the usual channel," Zoltan added, "the people of Sevlar will never suspect that the lead weather gods' faces and voices in those videos are computer-generated."

"This is not good," Mr. Winchester said next. "Xavier will be able to spread all the propaganda he wants. He'll likely try to convince the whole population that WE are the enemy."

"Is there any way we can tap into the system and block those broadcasts?" Torin asked.

"Unfortunately not," Argon answered. "The system was designed to be 100% hacker-proof."

"Then I suppose we have no choice," Mr. Winchester announced, standing up from his rocking chair. "We have to go and rescue them. And time is of the essence."

"Speaking of time," Demetrius added. "When is this food supply ship supposed to return to Sevlar?"

"About two hours ago," Argon replied while checking his watch.

"Then you need to get back as quickly as you can," Demetrius said very logically. "Xavier will surely be monitoring and investigating anything out of the ordinary."

"You're right," Argon commented. "But since cargo ships often run behind schedule, I should be safe if I depart now."

CHAPTER 13

Once the cargo ship was safely on its way, they returned to working out the details of this upcoming rescue mission.

"What worries me most," Zoltan told everyone, "is that Xavier will notice our arrival the second our ships penetrate the stratosphere. If we can't rescue everyone and get them out quickly, Xavier's troops will have enough time to attack us. We'll be sitting ducks."

"I believe I can help us out of that conundrum," Vasilios mentioned. "Two of our ships have no transponders in them. They can land undetected."

"That's impossible," Maximillian remarked. "If a transponder is removed from a ship, that ship's engines don't work."

"Very true," Vasilios smiled. "But we managed to find a loophole. We didn't remove the transponder from the ship; We removed the ship from the transponder."

"Which means…?" Zoltan asked.

"Our engineers spent years disassembling two ships, piece by piece," Vasilios explained. "Then they carefully built both ships again, from scratch, without transponders."

"Why didn't you do that for all of your ships?" Maximillian inquired.

"Because of how demanding and time-consuming it was to do only those two," he replied. "Plus, we never imagined we would need a fleet of stealth vessels."

"Peter," Mr. Winchester said from across the room. "Can you get all your friends here first thing tomorrow morning?"

Peter gulped. (He had just had a fight with Neil. Bradley had been in a car accident. And he hadn't talked to Nicola or Claire in ages…)

"I'll round up as many as I can," Peter answered. "Can someone fly me home so I can start making phone calls?"

CHAPTER 14

Unfortunately, gathering his team was going to be a lot more challenging than it had been in the past.

Bradley was definitely out this time. He desperately wanted to help, but the doctor had given Peter's mom strict instructions that Bradley was to rest at home for at least a few days, just in case his concussion was worse than they thought.

For some bizarre reason, the person Peter called first was Claire. He had a short (but pleasant) chat with her, and she emphatically offered to help. When Peter told her he hadn't phoned Nicola yet, Claire said she would do that for him, as the two girls were fairly close these days. (But Neil's name was not brought up by either Peter or Claire...)

Peter somehow convinced himself that having Neil on their team wasn't necessary this time. (Or maybe Peter was just trying to avoid another confrontation?)

"No Neil, no Brad," Peter mumbled to himself. "I need one more person."

"Hey Pete," Bradley said loudly, walking into Peter's room—almost like he had read his brother's mind—unannounced. "Take Sophia."

The thought of bringing his little sister into this "rescue mission" had never even crossed Peter's mind. (But she wasn't exactly a "little kid" anymore, seeing as she was almost 14. She was also quite strong and athletic. Plus, and most importantly, she had been doing riddles with Peter for her entire life, so she would undoubtedly fit into their crew.)

* * *

"Sophia," Peter said while knocking on her door. "You got a minute?"

"Hold on!" she replied.

Peter heard her say something to whoever she was talking to on the phone, and then she hung up and yelled, "Okay, come on in!"

"How's Anita?" Peter asked (figuring his sister had been chatting with her best friend again.)

"That wasn't Anita," she answered. "It was Brock."

"Brock?" Peter asked back. "Who's Brock?"

"My soon-to-be boyfriend," she smiled. "But I'm going to play hard-to-get for a little while longer, just to make sure he really likes me."

Imagining his "baby sister" with a boyfriend

was not an easy task. But Peter did have to admit that she was old enough to be hanging out with boys.

* * *

Although he had expected it was going to take a lot of time (and evidence) to convince Sophia about the reality of all the weather god stuff, that was not the case at all.

Sophia liked, and trusted, Peter. (He had always played games and sports with her when she was little, plus he regularly helped her with homework as she got older.) She knew the last thing her brother would do was lie; If he needed her help, she was in.

CHAPTER 15

"You guys sure are up early," Peter's mom said to her three kids when they were all at the breakfast table a little before seven the next morning.

"Early to bed, early to rise," Bradley commented. "Isn't that what you are always telling us?"

Their mom put her hands on her hips and glared at them. "Very funny," she said. "You three had better behave yourselves today."

"Behave ourselves?" Sophia asked. "What are you talking about?"

"Did all of you forget," she said next, "that your dad and I are spending the day with Uncle James and Aunt Lindsey. We are meeting at your dad's golf club for breakfast at eightish, then going to an outlet mall for the day, followed by dinner and a show after."

"So if you hold a massive party here," their dad joked, "make sure you kick everyone out and clean the mess up before we get back at 10:30 tonight."

"And then start packing your bags to move out," their mom added, laughing. "As that's what your punishment will be if you are stupid enough to invite people over."

* * *

"Looks like I can come after all," Bradley smiled the minute his parents left at half past seven.

"It's too risky," Peter told him. "You never know when or if you might start showing concussion symptoms."

"Do you think I'm going to let my little brother and sister risk their lives?" Bradley went on. "While I sit on my butt watching TV? No way."

No response...

"If something happened to either of you," he went on, "I would never be able to forgive myself. Look, I'll be fine. And DO NOT mention anything about my accident to Zoltan, Mr. Winchester, or anyone else, okay?"

CHAPTER 16

When the five teenagers showed up at Mr. Winchester's shed at eight thirty, they were blown away by the massive fleet of over 30 ships awaiting their arrival.

"You are, no doubt," Mr. Winchester said politely while shaking Sophia's hand, "the intelligent and imaginative Sophia. The one we have heard so many great things about."

Sophia giggled. "I suppose I have been doing Pete's puzzles for, like, forever," she commented. "But he's a million times better at them than me."

"Where's Neil?" Maximillian asked.

That was a question that Peter had been expecting (but had yet to prepare an appropriate reply for.)

"He couldn't come," Nicola quickly said, sensing that Peter looked uncomfortable. "But luckily, Sophia is filling in for him."

"Why are ALL the ships powered up?" Peter asked Zoltan. "I thought only two had no transponders."

"My entire fleet is coming along," Vasilios answered. "We will hover above the atmosphere, just out of detection range."

"Um... okay," Peter mumbled.

"We want to be there just in case the *rescuers* suddenly become *rescuees,*"Vasilios mentioned.

* * *

Mr. Winchester had a list in his hand that he had just finished making changes to. "Here's who will go in each of the two undetectable ships," he told Peter.

Vessel 1:

Cynthia (pilot)
Claire
Nicola
Zoltan
Demetrius

Vessel 2:

Torin (pilot)
Peter
~~*Neil*~~ *Sophia*
Bradley
Leonardo

Peter knew that they were going to be bringing

Demetrius (since his experience as a lead weather god would come in handy), but he certainly wasn't expecting to see Mr. Winchester's name on the list.

"You shouldn't be coming," Peter told him, rather directly.

"Peter," Mr. Winchester smiled. "I appreciate your concern, but I'm afraid I must be part of this mission. I taught problem-solving at the academy for years, and Dendaxtra will be filled with mind-boggling challenges."

"Your mind may be sharp," Nicola commented. "But, and no offense, your body isn't physically up for this."

"Not to worry, Nicola," the old man grinned. "If I'm too slow, Bradley can always piggyback me."

"Of course I can, dude," Bradley laughed, high-fiving Mr. Winchester.

CHAPTER 17

"Mr. Winchester," Peter asked when they were about two-thirds of the way to Sevlar. "Did Demetrius tell you the details about HOW people were injured or killed at Dendaxtra?"

"He claimed he only knew *how many* were hurt or killed," Mr. Winchester replied. "But he might have told me that just to spare us from the gory details."

"Oh," Peter said back. "What exactly were those numbers?"

"He wouldn't tell me," Mr. Winchester said to his friend. "But by the sad expression on his face, I can only assume that the number was very high..."

* * *

As the two ships entered Sevlar's atmosphere, nerves soared and heartbeats sped up. Demetrius was giving Cynthia specific directions to get them to the location of this hidden test site. And Torin, who was piloting the other ship, followed close behind.

Before landing near the entrance, Demetrius instructed Cynthia to fly to the opposite side of the mountain.

"Now reduce our altitude until we are about 100 meters from the base," he said. "Over there, by that patch of trees."

Then he pointed at what looked like a huge pile of boulders.

"See that?" he said. "That was the tunnel the lead weather gods used to go in so they could view the tests while they were being done. Xavier has caved that tunnel in, and that means the only way we can rescue them today is by completing the challenges to reach where they are being held captive."

The communication channel with the other ship was open, and Torin quickly asked, "Were you expecting this?"

"Unfortunately, yes, I was," Demetrius replied.

* * *

The ships touched down outside the entrance, and everyone stepped off.

"As we discussed earlier," Peter said to everyone, "this is where we split up into three teams. Mr. Winchester, Zoltan, Sophia, and I will go into Dendaxtra and get started on the challenges. Demetrius and Claire are with Torin. Brad and Nik with Cynthia. Take the two ships, carry out your assignments, and then get back here as fast as you can."

"And before we start," Zoltan added. "Everyone please check that the emergency call button attached to the back of your belt is turned on. If you get into trouble, push that button, and Vasilios' ships will immediately come to get you."

"Any questions?" Peter asked.

"Just one, Pete," Bradley replied. "Could you please explain why you don't look scared right now?"

CHAPTER 18

"Look at this," Peter said to Zoltan, Mr. Winchester, and Sophia while pointing to a plaque mounted just beside the entrance to the caves.

Assessment Zone
All four challengers are to enter
together.

"Why did they do these tests in groups of four?" Zoltan asked. "Weather gods are always sent to planets alone, aren't they?"

"That probably gave the lead weather gods a way to compare each challenger to the others," Mr. Winchester guessed. "To see who was making the decisions and who was just following along."

The short tunnel led them to a wooden door, which had partially rotted and was covered in thick moss. This time, the plaque was mounted on the door.

Patience and Bravery Assessment

"No instructions?" Peter commented.

"I suppose they might have given something to the challengers back in the day," Mr. Winchester said. "Or possibly not. We can't really know, and Demetrius didn't mention anything about that."

"Pete?" Sophia—looking quite nervous—said to her brother. "Are these going to be harder than all the games and puzzles you used to make for me?"

Sensing his sister's fear, Peter elected to answer in the most encouraging way he could. "I doubt it," he said supportively. "You got this."

She held her elbow up to Peter and started laughing. The two did an "elbow high-five," something they used to do when they were little.

"Time to get to work," Peter smiled.

They walked through the door into a dimly lit, stone chamber: a rectangular room not much bigger than Peter's bedroom.

"There must be an exit in here somewhere," Zoltan commented. "Or at least a button or something to reveal a hidden door."

As soon as the last one in their group (Mr. Winchester) was in, he closed the door behind them. They heard a loud click as if something had just been turned on.

"Guys! The floor is moving!" Sophia yelled in a

panic. "It's slowly rising!"

Peter knelt on the ground and put his face close to one corner. Sure enough, the floor was slowly rising: meaning if they didn't find the exit in the next few minutes, they would be flattened like pancakes!

Sophia started running from wall to wall, pushing in random places in the hope of finding some hidden button that would save their hides.

Mr. Winchester and Zoltan—two veteran puzzlers—took a calmer approach. They began looking around the *gradually shrinking room* for clues or hints.

There wasn't anything written on any of the four walls, but there was still a chance that the placement of the stones on those walls might form a symbol, number, or something helpful.

"What's that?" Zoltan said, pointing to a small device mounted in one of the top corners. "Looks like a tiny camera."

"That must be how the lead weather gods watched what happened in here," Mr. Winchester remarked.

Realizing that they needed to coordinate their efforts a little better, Peter decided to take over, and he doled out some instructions.

"Guys," he said. "Let's sit down, backs to each other, and face one wall each."

Following Peter's plan of action, they all quickly got in position. (Well, Mr. Winchester didn't move that fast...) They were now in the center of the room, backs touching each other.

And then the floor suddenly stopped rising!

"Yes!!" Peter said, raising his arms in the air.

But the instant he moved, the floor began moving again!

"What the...?" Sophia said loudly. "I don't get it."

"This is a very old contraption," Zoltan mentioned. "There are probably some chips or cracks in the cogs, making it stutter a bit."

And then it stopped moving again.

"Guys," Peter instructed everyone. "Sit as still as you can for a minute: I have a theory I wanna check."

For the next sixty seconds or so, no one moved other than to blink, inhale, or exhale.

"I think that camera has a motion detector in it," Peter said, moving nothing other than his lips. "When we move, it triggers the floor to rise."

"Let's test that out, then," Zoltan said, standing up quickly.

The floor once again moved, but as soon as Zoltan froze in his stance, it stopped again.

"This means we have just bought ourselves as much thinking time as we want," Peter smiled.

* * *

Once they had all finished their visual scans of the four walls (which amounted to nothing), they decided to check the floor and ceiling. Since Zoltan was already standing, he slowly leaned his head down so he could examine the floor. And Mr. Winchester tilted his head up to check the ceiling.

* * *

"Nothing," Zoltan said. "At least not to the naked eye."

"Same here," Mr. Winchester said about the ceiling.

"How about this?" Sophia suggested. "The floor has moved up so much that we should be able to touch the ceiling now. If Zoltan goes over and holds something in front of the motion sensor, then the rest of us can move freely and check things more carefully."

"Nice," Peter grinned. "Zoltan, go for it."

Zoltan required a few steps to get to the corner, meaning the floor moved up ever so slightly as he strode over there.

He used his big palm to block the sensor. "Okay, stand up, and let's see what happens," he told everyone.

The floor remained fixed!

They pushed, rubbed, and scratched just about every square inch of the ceiling, floor, and all four walls... to no avail... (What were they missing?)

"Is your arm tired from holding it up there for so long?" Peter asked Zoltan.

"Nah, I'm good," he replied.

* * *

"Pete," Sophia said after a few silent minutes. "I probably don't know what I'm talking about, but... well, I remember how so many of the riddles you used to make often had a clue hidden within a few simple words."

"Words?" Peter asked back. "But there's no written hint or clue for this puzzle."

"What about the words written on the plaque outside the door?" she said next. *"Patience and Bravery Assessment."*

"Oh, I see where you're going with this," Mr. Winchester commented. "You think that rearranging those letters might spell something?"

"Actually," she answered. "I think the words *Patience* and *Bravery* might BE the hints."

"Do explain, young lady," Mr. Winchester said curiously.

"Patience would infer the fact that we need to, um... *wait* for something," she replied. "And for bravery... well, brave people don't shy away from fearful situations."

"Hold on," Peter said to his sister. "Are you

suggesting that we just let the floor rise and rise until something happens?"

"I know it sounds crazy," she answered, "but yeah, I think it's worth a shot."

"Too risky," Zoltan said, stating his opinion bluntly.

"Then let's do this," Sophia continued, acting much more mature than her years. "We let it go up and up until we have to lie flat on the ground. If nothing happens, then once it's getting close enough to crush us, Zoltan puts something in front of the sensor to block it, and we all slither out the door we came in originally. That door goes all the way up to the ceiling, so we can use it to get out of here if necessary."

One meter from the ceiling.

80 centimeters from the ceiling.

60 centimeters from the ceiling.

45 centimeters from the ceiling.

All four, lying on their backs now, looked up at the stone ceiling that was getting closer and closer to squashing them.

Zoltan's nerves took over, and he blocked the sensor (stopping the rising floor.)

Peter had to take a few deep breaths, as this

was a claustrophobic person's nightmare.

"I say we let it go up another ten centimeters," Sophia suggested.

Zoltan guessed the distance between his face and the ceiling. "Maybe five or six at the most," he advised. "We are not as thin as you."

Heart pounding, Zoltan uncovered the sensor. They tensed up as they got closer to being flattened.

"I'm stopping it now!" Zoltan yelled.

"Not yet!" Sophia told him. "Wait a couple more seconds!"

Click.

The floor stopped rising!

...

Clank. Grind.

The floor started lowering! (And it was going down a lot faster than it had risen.)

As it sunk, they first got on their hands and knees, and later stood up. When the floor was flush with its original position, it didn't stop there, it continued sinking lower and lower.

"Look!" Sophia exclaimed. "There's the exit!"

The floor ended up stopping about a meter

below its original position, and there was a crawl-size hole in one of the walls.

"Awesome work!" Peter said, high-fiving her.

"You're a natural," Mr. Winchester added, commending Sophia's brilliance.

"Runs in the family," she smiled while leading their team through the low and narrow tunnel.

CHAPTER 19

Demetrius, Torin, and Claire's team (which had been tasked with the very challenging mission of sneaking into the lead weather gods' meeting room) prepared to exit their ship, which they had set down in a small field in the city's outskirts.

"What I don't understand," Torin said to Demetrius, "is why we don't just use one of the hidden underground tunnels? You know, like the one Peter and Zoltan used to get to the archives."

"At first, I did give that option some consideration," Demetrius answered. "But Xavier's men will be guarding all six of those tunnels. The chance of us succeeding would be nil."

"So what's Plan B?" Claire asked.

"I don't think I'm confident enough to call it *Plan B,*" Demetrius replied, "as my other idea might be more rumor than fact."

"What do you mean?" Torin asked him.

"When I was appointed to my post as a lead

weather god," Demetrius went on, "it was briefly explained to me that a secret entrance to the meeting chamber existed."

"Where?" Claire inquired.

Demetrius laughed. "Based on what you know of Sevlarians, I'm sure you won't be surprised by this: We were not told the hidden entrance's actual location, we were only informed of where we needed to go to determine how to find it."

"I'm confused," Claire admitted.

"Each new lead weather god was read the following," Demetrius—having memorized these lines to perfection—continued. *To find the location of the hidden entrance, go to the roof of the Beldorf Museum. It will point you in the right direction.*"

Claire couldn't help but shake her head. "You silly Sevlarians," she commented. "Can't you do anything straight-forward?"

* * *

Because of Peter's successful ruse on his previous mission to Sevlar—the trick when he fooled the library staff into thinking he was a weather god by wearing a cloak—they decided to use the same plan again today with Claire. She had borrowed an old one from Aurora.

It was a beautiful sunny day, meaning most people chose to head to places like parks (instead of museums), so they were seen by very few Sevlarian citizens while walking in.

All public museums on Sevlar were free for visitors, so staff were only there to answer questions and give tours.

Demetrius knew their cloaks would attract some attention, so he had thought up something simple to tell the staff at the desk.

"We just came in to relax for a while, not to do research," he said politely to the nervous-looking young man behind the counter. "How do we get to the roof of this beautiful building?"

"Uh, uh..." he responded, shocked to be so close to three weather gods. "This old building has no elevator, but the stairs are right over there." Sensing his chance to converse a little more with these three important people, he then asked, "Shall I take you up?"

"We'll be fine on our own," Torin said, smiling. "As my friend here just mentioned, we have only dropped by to kick back and take it easy."

* * *

There was, thankfully, no one else on the roof of this ancient 4-story concrete building, which (although it was a beautiful piece of architecture), likely wasn't up to snuff when it came to safety.

"Um..." Claire said once they had been on the roof for a minute or two. "Where should we start looking?"

"What have we here?" Torin commented, squatting down beside the big bronze compass which had been built in the center of the roof (so visitors knew which way was north.) "This compass sure *points* at something, doesn't it?"

They faced the exact direction of the north-pointing arrow, walked to the edge of the roof, and rested their arms on the barrier that had been built to prevent people from falling off.

"The only thing of significance north of if us is, uh… fields," Claire said. "Does that mean a tunnel is hiding out there in the fields?"

"Unlikely," Demetrius answered. "The weather god chambers are southwest of the museum, not north. I would suspect the hidden entrance is quite close to the fortress itself."

CHAPTER 20

Cynthia, Bradley, and Nicola had an equally difficult (but infinitely riskier) task to accomplish: They needed to get very close to Xavier's prison cell.

* * *

The one thing that didn't seem to make sense was the reason Xavier elected to stay in prison. Although he had been incarcerated by the Sevlarian government, the bulk of the prison staff were working for him now, so they could technically let him walk out at any time...

Mr. Winchester had a theory as to why they decided not to do that: As long as Xavier remained in prison, Sevlarians would continue with their daily lives as usual, (meaning Xavier could continue his recruiting efforts unabated.)

Since Torin had previously lived on the prison compound as a spy, he knew the ins and outs of its entire operation. (But he couldn't be on their team today because his face would be easily recognized.)

Torin had, thankfully, come up with a scheme that could get a couple of people close to Xavier.

* * *

Cynthia (who was also too recognizable) had to keep her distance from the prison guards. She was currently hiding behind a patch of trees, about half a kilometer west of the gate.

"Are you two sure you can do this?" she said into her communicator to Bradley and Nicola.

Nicola was terrified, so Bradley pressed the button to reply. "Yeah, we're game," he answered. "Just don't overdo it, eh?"

* * *

The plan Torin had concocted involved using a common protocol that had to be followed during any tectonic event of a specific magnitude or higher. This special prison—which was built for its one and only prisoner, Xavier—was a public institution, and therefore had to follow earthquake protocol to the letter.

* * *

"Time to rock and roll," Cynthia smiled, getting ready to shake the ground. "Well, maybe just *rock.*"

Since the prison was reasonably close to a fault line, an earthquake would, at first glance, be interpreted as natural (as opposed to man-made or artificial.) She needed to get it over a magnitude of 6.0, but without an accurate way to measure this, all she could do was guess.

"Nice," Bradley grinned as the ground began shaking under him.

Nicola grabbed Bradley's hand and squeezed hard. "Brad," she said. "I'm scared."

The prison's earthquake alarm sounded and the safety systems automatically kicked in. Xavier's cell remained locked, but all the other doors immediately unlocked and opened. The staff then quickly and orderly proceeded out the exit.

"Okay, we're up," Bradley said to Nicola. "Can I have my hand back?"

The two teenagers slipped out from the rock outcropping they were hiding behind and dashed into the prison. (The prison staff had congregated far enough away that they didn't notice anything.)

* * *

"Brad?" Nicola said while following him through the hallways.

"Shh..." he said back. "We have no idea if anyone is still—"

Fa-thud!

Bradley had just fallen over!

Nicola, panicking, started shaking him. "Brad! Brad!" she said. "What happened?"

Bradley tried to open his eyes, but he looked dopey.

"Did you trip?" she asked. "Or hit your head on something?"

Bradley, appearing to be very dizzy, didn't reply...

"You're having concussion symptoms, aren't you?" she asked him.

Bradley, still half out of it, nodded.

"Then I guess I'll have to do this on my own," she mumbled angrily. "When you are feeling okay enough to stand up, don't go anywhere. Just wait here, I'll be back for you on my way out."

CHAPTER 21

The 70-by-70-centimeter tunnel was awkward and uncomfortable for Peter, Zoltan, and Sophia to crawl through, but downright awful for poor old Mr. Winchester's ancient knees and aching back. And since there wasn't enough space to help him, all they could do was encourage him to proceed at his own pace.

When the old man finally emerged from the long tunnel—a good two minutes after the rest of the team—he was all smiles. "Nothing like reliving one's youth, right?" he laughed.

Zoltan helped him up and Peter assisted by hitting the dirt off his trousers.

This chamber, which by the looks of it was about three times the size of the previous one, also had a small plaque in it, which this time was part of the floor. Sophia squatted down to read its contents.

Perfection Assessment
(One attempt only)

On the far side of the chamber, there was a solid-looking door with three dials on it. Peter and his sister quickly jogged over to take a closer look.

"Each dial can be set from numbers *1* through *9!*" Sophia said loudly so that Mr. Winchester and Zoltan could hear her.

"Reminds me of what banks use on their vaults," Peter commented.

"Pete, what's 9 to the power of 3?" Sophia asked.

"729," Peter answered right away. (Well, it did take him a few seconds to calculate that...)

"So that's how many possibilities there are, right?" she asked next.

"You got it," Peter answered.

Since this room was quite a fair size, it also had three pillars, which must have been built to give extra support to the rock ceiling.

As Peter and Sophia were walking back to join their two Sevlarian teammates, the room suddenly got a lot brighter.

"Cool," Sophia commented. "Feels like Christmas."

The three pillars, which at first glance appeared to be nothing more than simple stone ones, actually had tons of tiny lights mounted on them, which were flashing on and off very quickly.

"Three pillars, three dials," Zoltan commented.

"Not only that," Mr. Winchester added. "But the relative positions make it quite clear which one corresponds to each dial. Let's attack this from more than one front. You three go and look at the pillars up close. I'll stand back here and view them from a distance."

* * *

It was, of course, impossible to look at the entire surface of a round pillar at one instant; The best they could do was stand at one vantage point, examine it for a bit, and then take a few steps around it and inspect again.

"I've got two ideas that might help us here," Sophia suggested soon after. "One is to count the number of lights on each pillar. And the second is to see if the positioning of the lights looks like the outline of a number."

"Let's start by checking your second idea," Zoltan said. "I was thinking along the same lines myself."

Zoltan loudly announced their plan of attack to Mr. Winchester, who gave them a thumbs up.

* * *

"I've just gone around my pillar twice," Peter said a few minutes later, "but I don't see anything that looks even vaguely like a number."

"Me neither," Sophia said next. "Zoltan?"

"Nope," he replied. "Time to start counting lights, I guess."

* * *

Mr. Winchester, meanwhile, walked over to the locked exit. He wanted to make sure there wasn't some kind of clue written on the door itself. (Weather god tests could be quite tricky, so he didn't want to leave any stones unturned.)

* * *

"61," Peter—on the left-most pillar—said. "Assuming I didn't count some twice."

"Mine's got 75," Sophia said next.

"Sorry guys," Zoltan told them both. "I've gotta do a recount, I lost track of where I started."

* * *

"52," Zoltan said once he was done. "Now let's switch pillars and double-check."

The first pillar definitely had 61, and the second, 75. But when Sophia checked the third one—the one Zoltan had originally counted—her total came to 54.

"Let me count, too," Peter said, deciding to be the tie-breaker.

* * *

"54," he said a couple of minutes later.

Before Peter had a chance to reach into his backpack for pen and paper, Sophia handed her set to him.

"You two sure are a lot alike!" Zoltan laughed.

61
75
54

"Pete, pass me that for a sec," Sophia said, getting ready to add to his notes.

61: $6 - 1 = 5$
75: $7 - 5 = 2$
54: $5 - 4 = 1$

"What do you guys think?" she asked them.

"Leonardo," Zoltan said, calling him over. "What's your opinion on Sophia's deduction?"

"Very intriguing," the old man commented once he had looked at her notes. Then he walked over to the pillars to look at them closely for the first time. "When counting the totals, did you also count the lights that appear to be burnt out?"

"Yup," Peter replied.

"But maybe we should consider this," Mr. Winchester said next. "Maybe those lights aren't burnt out. Perhaps they are purposely turned off."

* * *

A quick (but careful) recount of the pillars revealed that the first one had 2 non-working lights, the second had 8, and the third had 4.

"2, 8, 4," Peter said. "That gives us a second possible combination."

"But to be completely honest," Zoltan commented next. "I still like our first assumption better. I think some lights are just malfunctioning because this place hasn't been maintained for so long."

"If all of us are in agreement, then," Mr. Winchester announced. "Let's set the dials to Sophia's original idea of 5, 2, and 1." He smiled. "And hope we are right…"

"Hold on," Peter said, jogging back to the entrance. "I wanna look at them from over here."

* * *

"Nah, nothing," Peter said while speed-walking back a minute later. (But he was looking at his notes instead of where he was headed, and somehow managed to trip over his own two feet!)

He dropped the pen and paper so he could use his hands to break his fall. But since he was right in front of one of the pillars, instead of putting his hands down, he put them out. He was able to get his palms on the pillar (saving himself from a painful fall.)

"Are you okay, Peter?" Mr. Winchester asked.

"Yeah, I'm fine," he replied. "The only thing I hurt was my pride."

Sophia was staring, eyes wide open, looking shell-shocked.

"Pete," she said with a very inquisitive expression. "When you fell into the pillar, it twisted a little. Did you notice?"

"Twisted?" Peter asked back. "Really?"

Sophia walked up and put her hands on the pillar. "Look," she announced, showing how she could make all the lights on it rotate in one direction. "The lights aren't built into the pillars, they are mounted on sleeves that encase the pillars, and those sleeves can easily be rotated."

Zoltan and Mr. Winchester were unsure of what to say or suggest. But instinct took over for Peter. "Mr. Winchester," he said. "Go stand by the entrance again."

(Even though he was the most senior, Mr. Winchester knew when to listen and do as instructed.)

"Now what?" the old man asked, once in position.

"We're going to spin these things as fast as we can," Peter explained.

"Umm… okay?" Mr. Winchester replied, a little confused.

"Guys, we have to get these things spinning really, really fast," Peter said. "Let's do them one at a time."

With all three standing around the left-most pillar, they began swatting it with their open palms over and over, watching it go faster and faster.

And even faster.

"Brilliant!" Mr. Winchester exclaimed. "The lights are forming the number *7!*"

"Yes!!" Peter cheered, jumping for joy.

They did the same for the middle and the right pillars, which (once spinning at the appropriate rates) unveiled a *3* and *9* respectively.

The old man walked up to his *huffing and puffing* teammates, and gave them all high-fives. "That was magnificent!" he exclaimed. "How did you even think of that?"

"You can thank my science camp teacher from two summers ago," Peter smiled. "We did this cool experiment where we created a spinning device with pulsating lights on it. When the lights were pulsated in a specific order, and the spinning set to a specific speed, the flashing lights could be made to look like shapes, or letters, or numbers."

"I think I saw a clock in a store once that did the same thing," Sophia added.

They walked up to the door and set the dials to 7, 3, and 9.

"Okay, sis," Peter smiled. "Pull the lever down and open up this sucker!"

Creak.

"It worked! It's open!" she cheered.

Sophia bolted through first, followed by Zoltan, Mr. Winchester, and finally Peter.

"I thought these challenges were all supposedly dangerous," Peter remarked, laughing a little. "That one certainly wasn't."

"Uh, Pete," Sophia—who was first to the next challenge—said. "Be careful what you wish for…"

CHAPTER 22

"Perhaps that contraption over there can help us," Claire said to Demetrius and Torin while pointing at the sightseeing telescope on the south side of the roof.

They walked over to this "device," which had most likely been installed up here to give visitors the opportunity to look around more closely at their beautiful city.

"The ones on Earth usually cost a quarter or a dollar to use for a minute or two," Claire mentioned. "How much are these?"

Demetrius started laughing. "People have to pay a fee for the privilege of looking at their own city?" he asked. "How crazy is that?"

"If we are lucky," Torin said next, "there is some marking up here on the roof to tell us where to aim this thing."

Claire put her eyes up to the telescope and twisted the knob to get it in focus. "Wow, this sure has strong magnification," she commented.

Then she put her hands on the side of the heavy apparatus, to see how much it could swivel.

"Looks like it covers about a 60-degree swath," she said. "And it can also go up and down a little."

"That's probably so people who want to check out the mountains just beyond the city can do so," Torin mentioned.

* * *

Torin and Demetrius' inspection of the area near and around the telescope yielded nothing.

"So, um…" Claire mumbled. "How do we know where to aim it?"

"Let me have a gander through those," Demetrius said. "I'm pretty good at spotting things that are out of place."

* * *

Since there was no way for more than one person at a time to use the telescope, Claire and Torin walked over to one of the benches and sat down.

* * *

"I have spotted a fairly peculiar thing," Demetrius said a few minutes later. "Torin, come over and give this a go. I won't say what I found, though. I want you to look with a fresh pair of eyes."

* * *

"This is what you saw, isn't it?" Torin said to Demetrius a few minutes later, encouraging Demetrius to look through the lens on what he had focused it on.

"Yup," Demetrius smiled.

"Can I take a look, too?" Claire said as she walked over.

"Oh, I get it," she said after seeing what her two Sevlarian friends had noticed. "You're using the line Demetrius was given when he became a weather god: *It will point you in the right direction.* The antenna on that tall building over there has a ball on its top, which looks like a dot, or a POINT!"

"So the entrance must be over there," Demetrius commented.

"But that building is pretty far away from the fortress," Claire mentioned. "Didn't you both say the secret entrance would be much closer?"

Torin and Demetrius looked at each other and nodded in agreement.

"Then perhaps there is another *point* somewhere," Torin said. "Claire, see what you can find."

* * *

"Very interesting," she said about four or five minutes later. (Both Demetrius and Torin didn't hear her, as they had gone to sit down. They were discussing other ways to look at this confusing conundrum.)

"Come and check this out!" she yelled excitedly.

Demetrius (the senior of the two) looked

through first.

"I'm confused," he said. "Or maybe I accidentally bumped it and it's no longer aiming at the correct spot."

Claire quickly looked through again. "Nope, that's exactly what I found," she told her elderly friend.

"But all I can see is an intersection," Demetrius commented during his second viewing. "Crosswalks, streetlights, a few buildings..." Then he paused. "Ingenious! Torin, check this out!"

Torin didn't need long to see what all the excitement was about. In the center of the lens, he could see the street sign that was attached to the top of the intersection, labeled *Grey Point Avenue.*

"Cool... Grey POINT Avenue," he smiled. "But how could they hide an entrance in an intersection?"

* * *

The three took turns using the telescope to examine the area around the intersection. (They weren't in a huge rush, but they did need to get this solved fairly soon.)

"What have we here?" Torin said about five minutes into their inspection. It was his third turn and he had decided to take a different approach this time. "Claire, look at the building to the right of the street sign. Tell me what you see?"

"Hmm…" Claire said while looking through the lens. "Just an old 2-story brick building. Looks like a post office or bank or something, and it has mirrored windows."

"Now look at the mirrors, specifically the second one from the right," Torin said feverishly.

"Well…" Claire said, not sure how to describe the mirrors as anything other than *mirrors*. "Wait! I think I see it! That's, like, so cool!"

Demetrius was extremely eager to get a look at this for himself. Claire stepped aside to let him have a turn.

"How peculiar," the old man commented. "If one looks at the mirror carefully, we can see the reflection of the building on the opposite side of the street. Most importantly, we can see how some tiles on that building, just beside an alleyway, form a big number *3*. But what would a *3* indicate?"

"C'mon, Demetrius," Claire laughed. "Remember, you are looking at the reflection!"

Demetrius chuckled at his oversight. "And the mirror image of a *3* is an *E*," he exclaimed.

"*E* for entrance!" Torin cheered. "Which has to be somewhere in that alley!"

CHAPTER 23

Shortly after walking through the exit of their previous puzzle, Peter and his team found themselves standing at another locked door. To the door's left, there was a waist-high pedestal with a plaque on its flat top. And on one corner of the pedestal lay a small bell, similar to the ones Peter had used back in the Grade 6 handbell choir.

Speed Assessment

Weather gods are required to solve problems at a moment's notice. This test was designed to determine if you are capable of doing so.

Pick up the bell. The ringing sound will unlock the door and start the countdown, which is precisely five minutes.

If you don't walk through the exit before the time expires, then just turn around and go home, as you will have failed this assessment.

Peter quickly put his hand in front of the bell to block Sophia from picking it up.

"Hold on a sec," he told his sister. "Let's all take a bit of a breather before starting on this."

His whole team sat down on the stone floor, and Peter dug some snacks out of his backpack for everyone.

Other than the polite and courteous *"Here you go,"* and *"Thank you,"* comments, their pit stop was relatively quiet.

* * *

When their simple yet satisfying snacks and juice boxes were finished, Peter stuffed the garbage into his backpack, stood up, and put his hand on the doorknob. "Okay," he said to Sophia. "Grab the bell and ring it. Let's see what's waiting for us on the other side of this door."

She nervously picked it up and shook it a few times. The high-pitched ringing echoed loudly around the small space they were in, but the click of the door unlocking was easily audible.

* * *

The area they walked into was not a large chamber this time, but simply a long, narrow hallway.

"Woah," Zoltan said in shock.

There was something, utterly terrifying, blocking their way through: a wall of FIRE!

Even though there was about three meters between the entrance and where the fire was shooting up from the ground, the heat it was sending off made it feel like they were in a furnace.

Then the fire suddenly stopped.

"Anyone know wh—" Zoltan started to say.

But then the fire wall turned on again!

Then it stopped for a brief second.

And then restarted. (But this time, it looked like the fire wall was a little further down the hallway.)

"Pete, I don't like the looks of this," Sophia said, having just lost a great deal of her confidence.

"Anyone see the timer?" Zoltan—who was shielding his face from the heat—asked.

"Maybe there isn't a timer mounted anywhere," Mr. Winchester quickly replied. "They might have intentionally not included one to increase the level of pressure on those being tested."

While holding his backpack in front of him to block the worst of the heat, Peter edged closer and closer to the bizarre fire walls that kept starting and stopping, hoping to get a better idea of exactly what they were up against.

* * *

"Guys!" he yelled back to the rest of his team, who were still very close to the entrance. "There's a narrow gap in the floor that spans the width of the hallway. And I can see a metal pipe in it that runs—aargh!" He jumped back as the wall of fire blasted up and almost burned him. "And there are little holes on the top side of the pipe: I bet the pipe contains natural gas, and when blasted out through the holes, and lit, becomes a fire wall."

Peter paused.

Then he started counting.

Shortly after, he walked back and rejoined his team.

"Bad news, there isn't just one gap creating one fire wall," he explained. "There are six gaps in total, one after the other. And there is only, like, half a meter of floor between each gap."

As a team, they got as close as they could to the location of the first gap (without getting cooked like marshmallows on a campfire!)

"How much time left?" Sophia asked her brother.

"Oops," Peter reacted. "I forgot to start my watch."

"About four minutes," Mr. Winchester smiled while looking at his own timepiece.

They stood and watched as the six fire walls turned on and off in seemingly random order. Sometimes only one would be on, sometimes two at the same time. Some would stay on for less than a second, and others for close to three or four seconds.

"We need to figure out the pattern," Zoltan commented. "Then we will be able to jump over each gap when we know it will be off."

* * *

Spotting a pattern or order was always a fairly challenging task, but their current lack of time was going to make it brutally difficult right now: As the time constraint meant they couldn't watch things three or four times carefully to confirm the pattern...

* * *

"Two and a half minutes to go," Mr. Winchester said nervously. "Anyone?"

"1, 2 and 6, 4 and 3, 1 and 4, 2 and 5, 1 and 3 and 6," Zoltan said. "I'm pretty sure that's the order."

"Awesome," Peter smiled.

"But I didn't count how long each one stays on

for," Zoltan said next.

"That shouldn't matter too much," Peter told him.

* * *

The whole team walked up to a spot close to the first gap and stood side-by-side.

"I think I now understand why so many people were injured or killed doing these tests," Zoltan gulped.

"We'll be fine," Peter said. "And can you tell me the order again? I want to write it down."

1

2 and 6

4 and 3

1 and 4

3 and 5

1 and 3 and 6

Sophia was looking over Peter's shoulder as he wrote. "Pete," she said curiously. "Pass me that."

She quickly started crossing things out. "Check this out," she smiled, handing the paper back.

1

2 ~~and 6~~

~~4 and~~ 3

~~1 and 4~~

~~3 and 5~~

~~1 and 3 and 6~~

Peter gave her a high-five. "Nice!" he told his sister. "A super simple pattern hidden within a complex-looking one... Very tricky."

They edged a little closer, waiting for the instant the pattern would restart. Peter was looking back and forth between his list and the fire walls.

The 3 and 5 turned on and off.

Then the 1 and 3 and 6.

"Okay, the next set is about to start," he announced. "We gotta move like lightning each time."

The 1-fire wall blasted on, then turned off.

"Now!" Peter said loudly.

"Wait!!" Zoltan yelled, sticking his arms out to block everyone from moving. They all stumbled, but were able to quickly regain their balance and move back a few steps.

"What!?" Peter said, sounding irritated. "Why did you stop us? Now we have to wait for this entire set to finish."

Zoltan felt like snapping back at Peter, but knew that would just waste some of their precious time. "It's impossible to go across the way you are planning," he explained. "The distance between each gap isn't half a meter, it's more like 20 centimeters. That's not nearly enough space. If we go over the first gap, fire wall 2 will fry us when it turns on."

Peter crawled a little closer to inspect this point.

(Zoltan was right…)

"So now what?" he asked in a panic.

Sophia could see the terror in her brother's face, so she crawled up beside him and patted him on the back.

"Hey, Soph," he said sadly. "We are out of options."

She crawled over closer to the spot near the first fire wall.

It flared up.

And then shut off.

She quickly shoved her face into the gap and peered in.

Peter pulled her back as fast as he could. "What are you doing?" he screamed. "You're gonna get yourself killed!"

"Let go of me!" she yelled at him. Then she quickly stood up and bolted out the entrance.

"Peter," Mr. Winchester told him. "We've only

got a minute to go."

Sophia sprinted back in with the bell in her hand.

(The bell??)

"What on Earth are you planning on doing with that?" Peter asked her.

She ignored her brother's question.

The last fire walls of the cycle, the 1, 3, and 6, turned on and then off.

"Forty seconds," Mr. Winchester said nervously.

Peter grabbed Sophia's wrist. "Don't do something stupid," he scolded her.

She forcefully ripped her arm loose and then watched carefully as the new series started. The 1-fire wall burned brightly, then shut off.

She lay on her stomach—bell in hand—and stuck her hand (and part of her face) into the first gap.

"One down, five to go," she said a couple seconds later.

"What do you mean?" Peter questioned her. "What did you just do?"

The 2 and 6 fire walls turned on, then off.

Sophia then quickly did the same thing to the second gap.

"It's simple, Pete," she said while waiting for the 3-fire wall. "I'm using the bell to snuff out the pilot light in each gap. The gas can't be lit when the pilot light is off."

"Pilot light?" Zoltan asked.

"Ah..." Mr. Winchester grinned. "The fireplace at the community center has one of those: a tiny flame that continuously burns. When the gas is turned on, that flame ignites the gas, creating fire."

"But without that tiny flame," Zoltan added. "No fire!"

By the time those comments were done, Sophia had finished the 3 and 4.

"Are we doing okay for time?" she asked.

"I think so," Mr. Winchester answered. "Twenty seconds to go."

"Then get up here behind me," she ordered her three teammates. "As soon as I kill the pilot light for gap 6, run like stink for the exit!"

* * *

After snuffing out the 6, Sophia chased the rest of her team through the exit. Mr. Winchester then proudly announced, "We still have five seconds to spare!"

High-fives all around!

"And I guess we all know now that the plaque itself hinted at the solution," Zoltan laughed. "You know, the phrase *pick up the bell.* We were supposed to hold onto it."

"But we mistakenly put it back down right after ringing it," Peter added, "assuming we wouldn't need it for anything else."

"We are sure lucky Sophia spotted that slip-up in time," Mr. Winchester smiled.

CHAPTER 24

Claire, Demetrius, and Torin were now standing in front of the narrow alley next to the building with the big *E* on it.

The alley itself—which was simply a 1-meter gap between two old buildings—looked anything but special.

"I bet stray cats are the only living things that ever come down this dingy area," Claire mentioned as she followed Torin. "What exactly should we be looking for?"

Demetrius laughed a little from behind. "That question sure pops up a lot, doesn't it?" he said.

* * *

When they reached the end of the alley, which was about eleven or twelve meters in length, no one had spotted anything of importance.

"We're trying to find an entrance, right?" Claire commented. "Which would have to be on one of the building walls, or on the ground between them."

"Then maybe this is what we are after?" Demetrius remarked while pointing at the heavy, circular, steel cap on the ground (which if removed, would lead them to the sewer.)

"That can't be it," Torin said. "It looks exactly the same as all the other sewer caps in the city." Then he stopped and smiled. "Hiding it in plain sight? How interesting…"

Demetrius effortlessly conjured up a little tornado, which he used to lift the heavy disc up and off to the side. "Looks like nothing more than a sewer down there to me," he remarked. "Certainly smells like one."

"Only one way to find out, boys," Claire said boldly while starting down the ladder mounted inside. "Someone hand me a flashlight."

* * *

"It smells something awful down here," she announced from the bottom of the ladder. Even though she was plugging her nose with her free hand, it still made her gag.

"See anything?" Torin asked.

Claire quickly climbed back out, crawled a meter or two away from the hole, rolled on her back, and then finally started breathing again.

"Nope," she replied. "And that was, quite possibly, the grossest thing I have ever done."

Claire needed some time to recuperate from her disgusting mission down in the sewer, so Demetrius and Torin began looking around for other options.

* * *

"The outside walls of both buildings are bare," Demetrius said a few minutes later. "The only thing I can see is this little plaque near the back corner of the brick building."

"Plaque?" Torin asked.

"But it's nothing special or rare," Demetrius answered. "Just like all other buildings on Sevlar, the plaque was put there to show who owns the property."

Property owned by
Uspar Ltd.

Claire had gotten the worst of the stench out of her nostrils, so she walked over to check out the plaque as well.

"Maybe it's a big button?" she suggested while pushing it.

That attempt was, as she had expected, in vain.

* * *

As the three looked at the plain and boring plaque, Demetrius had a brainwave.

"Now hold on a second here," he said. "I wouldn't be surprised if the sentence we used to find this alley also tells us where the door is located."

"Which sentence?" Claire asked.

"It will point you in the right direction," Torin replied.

All three got to pondering how (or if) a clue was hiding somewhere in those words.

* * *

A couple minutes later, Demetrius smiled again. He put his ancient hands on the sides of the plaque and twisted the whole thing 90 degrees to the right.

"A twistable plaque?" Torin laughed. "Now that's a first."

Click.

And then a 70-centimeter gap opened in the wall!

"Yahoo!" Torin yelled. "But please explain how you knew to twist it."

"From these three words in the clue," Demetrius replied. *"Point, you, right."*

"Not following," Claire laughed.

"The word *you,"* he went on, "is pronounced the same as the letter *U.* And the word *point* can be a noun as well as a verb."

"Sorry, still not following," Claire repeated.

"Ah... You think it was telling us we had to aim the *points* of the letter *U* to the *right!"* Torin commented.

"What *U?"* Claire asked immediately after that.

"The capital U on the plaque," Torin laughed. "The U in Uspar Ltd."

"Bingo," Demetrius answered. "Now let's get in and out as fast as we can."

CHAPTER 25

Peter, Sophia, Mr. Winchester, and Zoltan didn't have to walk far before arriving at the entrance to the final test area. (The reason they knew it was the last one was that the door to this chamber—which was currently closed—had a *Final Assessment* plaque mounted on it.)

"Sophia," Peter said to his sister. "You are the only reason we made it this far. Why don't you open it for us?"

Sophia's eyes beamed with pride after hearing that remark, since she had spent her entire life thinking she would never, ever be even remotely close to Peter's intelligential ability.

She put her hand on the cold doorknob, twisted it, and pushed the heavy door open.

* * *

"Wow!" Zoltan subconsciously remarked while looking around.

"That word certainly does sum this place up," Mr. Winchester agreed. "I just wish this final assessment zone didn't look so much like a horror movie set."

The terrifying challenge they now had to tackle had both similarities and differences compared to some of the ones they had done in the past.

The finish line for this test was the easiest thing to recognize: an exit on the far side of the chamber.

And similar to the 9-bridge puzzle—the one Peter had created less than a year ago—getting to the opposite side of this huge chamber also involved getting to the first ridge (which was about one-third of the way across), then from there to the second ridge (about two-thirds of the way), and finally to the far ledge.

But unlike many of their previous challenges—which had required crossing over deep chasms—this time all three of the 2-meter gaps contained thousands of large spikes.

The tips of these upwards-facing spikes, which appeared to be about a meter in length, rose up from a platform that was half a body length below the level of the ledge they were standing on. (Thus, making the tips more or less flush with the entrance floor, ridges, and exit ledge.)

Peter knelt down and lightly touched the top of a spike with his right index finger. He was hoping to be able to tell his team that the points weren't that sharp, but his assumption had been

incorrect.

The spike pierced his skin immediately, and a small drop of blood appeared.

"I don't even wanna know how many lives this death trap took," Peter commented while standing up.

The spikes were not the only peculiar thing about this magnificent (in a bad way!) chamber.

The center of their ledge, and both of the ridges, each had a small, stone pedestal. And each of these pedestals had a crossbow resting on it. All three crossbows were loaded with a single arrow each, but there were no extra arrows anywhere.

The targets they would presumably be aiming for were simply holes—roughly one meter in diameter—on the side walls. There were five holes on the left, in random positions, labeled *1, 2, 3, 4,* and *5.* And the right wall had four holes, numbered *6, 7, 8,* and *9.*

"Anyone here ever fired a crossbow?" Mr. Winchester asked while inspecting (but not touching) the heavy weapon that some hunters love to use back on Earth.

"A regular bow? Yes, countless times," Zoltan answered. "But a crossbow? No, never."

"Look here," Sophia said next. "The top of this pedestal has a plaque with something written on it."

"Likely a clue," Demetrius commented.

"Which if we solve," Peter added, "should tell us which hole to shoot the first arrow in."

"And the pedestals on the two ridges," Mr. Winchester said next, "will both probably have clues on them as well."

Zoltan, the only one brave enough to touch the big weapon, lifted it up to allow his team to read the first of their three clues.

CHAPTER 26

Nicola had done her best to memorize the route Torin had shown her, but Bradley's sudden accident seemed to erase a large portion of that map from her head. (Luckily, she had Torin's sketch in her back pocket.) It was going to take a little longer to move (as she would have to pause periodically to check the map), but at least she'd be able to find Xavier's cell.

* * *

The elevator that was usually used to get to the location of Xavier's cell—deep below the surface—was unusable because the earthquake alarm had shut it off. That meant Nicola had to take the long, windy (and very dark) staircase. (And for some bizarre reason, there was no handrail: making what would normally be a simple task into quite a terrifying one...)

* * *

"Almost there," she whispered to herself. "All I have to do now is head down this hallway, punch in the code Torin gave me to open the final gate, make a left, and his cell should be right there."

Nicola did her best to tiptoe through the last part of the hallway, so that Xavier wouldn't hear her approaching.

"6 7 2 2 1 4 8 0," she said while punching the numbers in the small panel.

Instead of a green light—which would have indicated that it had just unlocked—a red one flashed.

"Calm down, Nik," she told herself. "You probably just botched something up when punching in the numbers."

She entered the code much more slowly this time.

But it flashed red again!

Now she was really worried. Torin had specifically explained that if the wrong code was entered three times here, that an intruder alert would be sent to all prison staff immediately. (And it didn't matter that the staff were all currently outside, since the alert would go to the device worn on their vests.)

"Torin told me they never changed the code while he worked here," she said to herself. "But I guess that doesn't mean they didn't change it after he left... But he also mentioned that although he used the code in various locations around the prison, that he never actually punched it in at this final gate."

Nerves skyrocketing, she lightly put her fingers up against the keypad again.

She closed her eyes and quietly wished herself good luck. "Please let this work," she pleaded. "Please."

Since her eyes were now closed, her other four senses became heightened.

"Hold on," she said before pushing the 6 (the first number in the code.) "These buttons feel like they have little bumps on them or something."

Bumps on the buttons?

"Braille!?" she said (a little louder than she should have.) "Just like elevator buttons back on Earth! I bet they put braille on these ones so the staff can still get through this gate even when it's pitch black down here."

Since braille was created to give blind people a way to read, 99.99% of people whose vision was fine were incapable of understanding it.

Nicola, however, had learned some very basic braille when she was in Grade 3. (The principal of their school had invited several people—with various disabilities and challenges—to come and give guest lectures to help increase kids' awareness of the challenges that some people face. The goal was to show kids how these brave individuals, despite their challenges, were leading full and active lives.)

She kept her eyes closed and felt around for the 6. "Bingo!" she said while opening her eyes.

But her finger was on the 8!

"How intriguing," she commented while shaking her head. "The digits *shown* on the buttons are red herrings. The braille markings indicate the real numbers of the buttons at this final gate. But I guess Torin wasn't high enough on the chain of command to be told that little secret."

Not wanting to be fooled by her eyes, she closed them again while hunting for each of the correct braille numbers in the code.

* * *

Click.

It unlocked!

Nicola slowly crept up to the T in the hallway and poked her head, ever so slightly, around the left wall.

* * *

Having seen exactly what Peter had sent her to investigate, she began retracing her steps. (She had to get out of this facility before anyone working here came back in!)

* * *

"What!?" she said, trying to figure out if she had mistakenly forgotten where Bradley had fallen. "I'm sure this is where he bit it."

"Brad," she said softly once. "Brad!" she called a little louder. "Where are you?"

No reply...

"I guess he went out on his own," she mumbled. "Man, that guy really can't sit still."

* * *

Nicola was lucky to have gotten out when she did, as she had only been back in her hiding space behind the rock outcropping for two minutes when the prison staff started to file back in. Whew!

* * *

As soon as the majority of the guards had re-entered, she bolted back to where Cynthia and Bradley would be waiting.

* * *

But Bradley wasn't there!

"Where's Brad?" Cynthia asked.

"He passed out shortly after we went in," Nicola replied while breathing heavily. "I told him I would get him on my way out, but when I came back, he was gone."

Cynthia stood up quickly. "Then I need to go in

and find him," she said. "He probably heard someone coming and hid in a broom closet or something. I have to go right now, before they lock the entrance."

"Should I contact Pete?" Nicola asked. "And tell him what I saw in there?"

"Not from here," Cynthia replied. "We have to wait until we get back to just outside the caves where Peter and the others are doing the tests. If you contact him now, Xavier's men will pick up the signal, and know we are here on Sevlar."

"Oh…" Nicola said.

Cynthia removed a device from her shirt pocket and punched something into it. "I just programmed the ship to take you back to the test site," she told Nicola. "Hop in, press this button, and autopilot will fly you there. After you land, wait for Torin's ship to arrive, and then contact Peter."

"What about you and Brad?" she asked, looking terrified.

"Don't worry, I'll find him," she said confidently. "Well, as long as he hasn't been taken hostage…"

CHAPTER 27

"Alright," Peter said to Sophia. "Let's hear the clue."

Did you know this??

The wannabe hero only sees,
What his eye tells him will bring him
fame.
But the true hero (whose level is above
all others with ease),
Knows that whether forward or
backward, some things still appear
exactly the same.

Wow, what does this clue refer to??

"Oh man," Peter said, rolling his eyes. "This has gotta be the most senseless hint I've seen to date."

"I'll second that," Zoltan added. "It's so bad

that I'm almost embarrassed to admit I'm Sevlarian."

"Embarrassed or not," Mr. Winchester told his former student. "We have to crack this one, and quickly."

"Lucky for us," Peter smiled. "My little sister here is a genius when it comes to poetry."

"Stop calling me *'little,'*" Sophia said (with enough of a grin to show she wasn't really angry.) "I'm almost as tall as you are now."

* * *

Over the course of the next five minutes, a few theories were suggested by Peter, Zoltan, and Mr. Winchester. But all of their ideas and interpretations were either far-fetched or too weak, so were quickly discarded.

Sophia had wandered a few paces away and (with her eyes now closed) was pondering how to decipher this bizarre riddle.

* * *

"Guys," she said after walking back to rejoin her team. "Tell me what you think of this?"

"Told you my little sis would come through," Peter commented.

Sophia glared at her brother and cleared her throat twice.

"Oops," Peter commented, getting ready to correct himself. "I mean my almost-as-tall-as-me sister."

"Ha ha ha," she groaned at her brother's

pathetic attempt at humor. "Anyway, one word in the clue struck me as being odd: the word *eye*. The phrase says *what his eye tells him*. But people have two eyes, not an eye."

"So that wasn't just an accidental grammatical error?" Zoltan asked.

"Here's my train of thought," she went on. "The word *eye* sounds the same as the capital letter *I*. And if you were to remove the horizontal lines from the top and bottom of a capital *I,* it would be just a single vertical line, which—"

"Looks just like the digit for number *1!*" Peter exclaimed.

"You're as brilliant as your brother," Mr. Winchester smiled.

"But let's consider other options first," Sophia continued, sounding like a born leader. "As that was just the first idea that popped into my head."

"Good call, boss," Peter remarked.

* * *

"What I've been doing," Mr. Winchester said a few minutes later, "was trying to look at the rhyme's meaning as a whole instead of hunting for specific oddities."

Did you know this??

The wannabe hero only sees,
What his eye tells him will bring him fame.

But the true hero (whose level is above all others with ease),
Knows that whether forward or backward, some things still appear exactly the same.

Wow, what does this clue refer to??

"Any luck?" Zoltan asked him.

"To be honest," the old man explained, "the first three lines are easy to understand, but the last one doesn't make any sense: *Knows that whether forward or backward, some things still appear exactly the same.*"

"I'm baffled by that part, too," Zoltan admitted.

"Ditto," Peter added.

* * *

Although no one verbalized their current state of mind, it was clear that all four were feeling desperate. They currently had only a single option: Sophia's idea to shoot for the *1,* and they didn't like it enough to settle on it.

Peter, unintentionally, began doing something he often did in his notebooks in class when he was bored to tears. He was tracing over each one of the letters in the clue (which he had written on a piece of paper a few minutes earlier.) He wasn't sure where this weird habit had come from, but he did recall watching his dad do it quite regularly while talking on the phone. (Maybe it ran in the genes?)

This subconscious habit of tracing over the letters was odd enough on its own, but what made it even weirder was that he didn't start from the first letter on a page, he usually started from the last.

Wow, what does this clue refer to??

"Question mark, question mark," Peter said softly to himself as his pencil went over each symbol and letter. "O, T, R, E, F, E..."

* * *

Thirty seconds later, he had almost reached the first word of the note's final sentence.

"T, A, H, W," he continued. "Comma, W, O, W." Then he giggled at the fact that he had just said the three letters that spell out *wow*.

Sophia was close enough to notice him laughing, and she asked, "What's so funny?"

"Sorry," he commented. "I'm laughing at myself for being so entertained by accidentally spotting a palindrome."

"Oh," she said, shaking her head at her brother's silliness. "You mean words like Bob, Mom, Dad."

Then Sophia's sarcastic expression turned into a celebratory one. "Palindromes!" she exclaimed. "A palindrome is the same whether read forward or backward!"

Peter slapped his forehead. "I can't believe I didn't think of that earlier!" he groaned.

Sophia looked over Peter's shoulder and scanned the note to see how many palindromes were in it.

* * *

"Six," she told her brother.

"Yup," Peter smiled. "Did, sees, eye, level, wow, refer."

"I guess that means I'm shooting for the 6?" Zoltan inquired while lifting up the crossbow.

"Sure you can hit it?" Mr. Winchester asked.

The *6* was, luckily, one of the closest of the nine holes. It was on the right wall, roughly at head level, and only about a meter ahead of their ledge.

Peter wondered for a second if Zoltan were allowed to walk up as close as possible to the hole before shooting the arrow, but when he noticed the crossbow had been chained to the pedestal, he realized that wasn't going to happen.

* * *

Zoltan got in a comfortable and sturdy stance, aimed carefully, and took a few deep breaths. The rest of the team remained behind him, so their presence wouldn't distract him from this crucial shot.

Swish.

In the 6!

As soon as the arrow had vanished into the hole, a grinding noise began. The sound was that of the first set of spikes slowly sinking into the floor below.

* * *

When the grinding stopped, they could see that these dangerous spikes had receded until they had completely disappeared into the surface below. Now all they had to do was slide off their ledge to the floor (which was just a flat surface with tons of small holes in it now), walk across, and then hop up onto the first ridge.

Since this drop was only a meter, Zoltan, Sophia, and Peter hopped down easily. Then they assisted old Mr. Winchester so he wouldn't hurt himself.

Getting up on the ridge was relatively easy as well. Zoltan went up first. Then Peter and Sophia helped boost Mr. Winchester (while Zoltan pulled on his arms.) And lastly, Peter and his sister climbed up, too.

"Nice aim back there," Peter told Zoltan, giving him a high-five.

"Not as nice as your sister's intellectual skills," Zoltan replied.

"I'm in full agreement there," Mr. Winchester smiled.

CHAPTER 28

Torin led their small group through the secret tunnel that would take them to the meeting room in the lead weather gods' fortress. (He wanted to move a lot faster, but seeing as Demetrius had two false hips, jogging was not an option.)

"Whoever built this tunnel sure did a good job," Demetrius commented once they had been moving through it for about a minute and a half. "There are very few places where rocks have crumbled from the walls or ceiling."

"Think we are the first people to ever use it?" Claire asked.

"We just might be," Demetrius answered.

* * *

"As quiet as possible from here on," Torin whispered to his team when he noticed they had almost reached the end of the tunnel. "Xavier's troops are not expecting us, but they will react if they hear something."

Both Torin and Demetrius figured the tunnel's

end would be similar to the beginning: meaning the exit would be another moving brick wall. But that was not the case at all.

"You have got to be kidding me," Demetrius said softly to the other two. "The secret pathway has always been hiding behind this?"

"That just looks like the back of a small, circular, bronze door," Torin said next.

"The back of it may be plain," Demetrius went on, "but the front of it, I assure you, is not. In fact, the front of that *bronze circle* is the crest of the original lead weather gods, from over two thousand years ago."

"But surely someone would have noticed that it could open?" Claire commented. "You know, when cleaning it or something?"

"That plaque is considered sacred," Demetrius told them. "Touching it, or even coming within a few steps of it, is strictly prohibited. That's one of the first things new lead weather gods are informed about."

"I'd love to hear more about this," Torin said, "but let's get our job out of the way first."

Torin removed a device from his bag that would hopefully help them accomplish their task without being noticed. It was by no means fancy, as they had bought it at an electronics shop before departing Earth.

"This is just like the spy cameras people use in movies all the time," Claire remarked. "A tiny camera on the end of a long, skinny tube."

"But we need to open the bronze door a crack in order to get the camera in," Torin commented. "Let's hope no one is close enough to it to notice."

"And let's also use some of this first," Demetrius said while reaching into his bag for a small can of oil. "The old hinge will probably squeak if we don't."

After some oil had been dripped on the rusty hinge, Claire (whose hands were the least shaky of the three) got ready to open it just enough to get the camera through.

Even though she only needed to move it a centimeter or two, she spent at least ten seconds doing this. They could now hear voices—although very faintly only—from inside the chamber.

Claire then slid the end of the tiny camera in, and adjusted the position of the flexible rod until it was facing in the right direction. Torin and Demetrius—who were looking at a small TV screen that was showing what the camera was picking up—tapped her on the shoulder and gave her a thumbs up. She carefully pulled the camera back, gingerly closed the bronze plaque so it was back in its original position, and then tiptoed backward.

CHAPTER 29

Knowing that time was not on their side, Zoltan quickly lifted the second crossbow so Sophia could read their next hint.

The possibilities are infinite.

"That's it?" Peter asked, sounding bothered (and a little surprised.) "Only four words? The last one was a long rhyme."

"Sorry, Pete," Sophia confirmed. "That's all that's written on this one."

"Let's try to maintain our composure here," Mr. Winchester calmly announced. "Frustration will be of no help at all."

"Here's my belly reaction," Zoltan started to tell everyone.

"Gut reaction," Sophia laughed, correcting him.

"Oops," Zoltan smiled. "Anyway, we shouldn't assume that the entire hint is on the plaque."

"What do you mean?" Peter asked (not clear about what Zoltan was getting at.)

"I guess what I'm trying to say," Zoltan went on, "is that just because the first plaque contained the entire first clue, it doesn't mean this one has the full second clue on it."

"I understand exactly what you want to point out," Mr. Winchester nodded. "As that was something I spent a good amount of time lecturing about in my advanced problem-solving classes. What Zoltan wants to say is this: If one falsely assumes that things always follow the same pattern, then that person is ignoring a plethora of possibilities."

Both Peter and his sister looked a little perplexed.

"In layman's terms," the old man smiled. "What we need to do here is this: Approach the second clue as if it were the first one. Do not think, in any way, shape, or form, that anything is linked or in common between the first and second hints."

"Is that your version of *layman's terms?*" Peter laughed. "But don't worry, I think I get it."

* * *

They split up and began checking each and every square inch of the pedestal, the crossbow, the surface of the ridge itself, and the walls on both sides. (There had to be more to the second clue around here somewhere!)

* * *

"No dice," a deflated Peter said a few minutes later, once he had completed the scan of his area. "Anyone?"

Zoltan and Mr. Winchester replied with a "No," and Sophia was shaking her head to indicate that she hadn't come across anything either.

"Back to the drawing board," Peter said sadly.

"Let's re-examine the clue on the plaque," Zoltan suggested.

The possibilities are infinite.

* * *

"Well, first things first," Mr. Winchester told everyone. "There are a total of 27 letters in this clue." Then he started to laugh a bit. "But I guess that doesn't tell us anything, now does it?"

"And can we assume that 6 is not the solution?" Zoltan asked his team. "Since we already used the *6.*"

"Most likely," Mr. Winchester agreed. "But we can't be sure."

For the next few minutes, all four were standing around the pedestal, each trying to contemplate this 4-word clue in his or her own way. (If you were to have walked into this room right now, you would have thought this scene to be the most boring and weird thing you had ever seen!)

* * *

"This kind of goes along with what Leonardo said earlier," Zoltan commented. "You know, about the number of letters: The word infinite has eight letters, think 8 could be right?"

"Hmm..." Mr. Winchester nodded while thinking about it. "Or perhaps we would benefit by trying to think of some things that are, well, *infinite.*"

"The mathematical value of pi continues infinitely," Peter said right away.

"And the number of times Brad has been yelled at by my mom," Sophia said next while smirking.

They unintentionally split up again and spent some time individually brainstorming *infinite* things.

* * *

"What's that?" Peter said to Zoltan (who was writing something down on a piece of paper.)

"You've never seen this before?" Zoltan asked back. "It's the symbol used when writing infinity."

"That looks nothing like the one we use on Earth," Peter told him. "Pass me your pen, I'll show you ours."

Directly under the complex-looking Sevlarian symbol, Peter wrote the one he had learned back in junior high.

∞

"Really? That's it?" Zoltan laughed. "Talk about overly simple. It looks all you did was turn the number 8 sideways."

Peter and Zoltan looked up at each other... And smiled simultaneously!

"Gimme five!" Peter said to his friend.

After slapping Peter's palm hard, Zoltan said, "There are now two things telling us the answer is 8: the fact that there are 8 letters in the word infinite, which to be honest was a little weak on its own. And now the much more meaningful fact that 8, when twisted sideways, looks like your infinity symbol!"

* * *

Even though they were on Sevlar, it was an undisputed fact that Sevlarians had been studying Earth customs as far back as anyone knew. (So not only had this test been originally designed to determine the deduction skills of those wanting to become weather gods, but it also provided a way to find out who had paid attention in class!)

* * *

Peter quickly brought the crossbow over to Zoltan and patted him on the back encouragingly.

"Shoot straight and true, my friend," he said in a deep and silly voice.

The 8-hole—which was also on the right wall—was not in as easy a position as the *6*... It was fairly high up on the wall, and almost two meters ahead of their ridge.

"Take your time, Zoltan," Mr. Winchester told him calmly. "If your pulse is racing, spend a few minutes deep breathing before you shoot."

* * *

Zoltan followed Mr. Winchester's advice, and when he felt he was as calm as he could get, he lined up and aimed at the *8*. He knew the most important thing was to not move anything other than his trigger finger when firing (to ensure it didn't fly off course.)

Dead center in the *8!*

Peter had been so nervous that he kept his eyes closed while Zoltan was getting ready, but the noise of the second set of spikes lowering into the ground made him realize that Zoltan had indeed hit the target. When he opened his eyes, Zoltan was strutting around, performing antics similar to what American football players do after scoring touchdowns.

Peter and Sophia happily joined in on the ridiculous show.

As soon as the spikes were completely gone, they moved to the second ridge.

(Only one more riddle to solve! And then the lead weather gods could be rescued!)

CHAPTER 30

"Look! The other ship is already back!" Claire said excitedly as Torin maneuvered theirs to land just outside the test site.

"Now all we have to do is confirm what they saw," Demetrius added. "And then we can contact Peter."

* * *

As soon as their ship door was open, Claire darted out, as she wanted to make sure Nicola and Bradley had made it back unscathed.

But no one was outside the other ship...

She ran up and banged on the unopened door a few times. "You guys in there!?" she yelled loudly.

* * *

On the big monitors, Nicola could see exactly what was going on outside, but she had no way to react. (The ship's voice recognition system wouldn't acknowledge her 'Open Door' command,

and she had no clue which button to push, since they were all unmarked...)

The only thing she could think of was to duplicate Claire. From the inside of her ship, she also banged hard on the door, and yelled, "I'm in here! But it's just me!"

* * *

The ship's thick insulation made what Nicola was saying indecipherable, but Claire easily heard the banging.

"Someone open up the door!" she called back to Demetrius and Torin. "I think they're stuck inside."

"I'm afraid I can't," Torin told her. "The door can only be opened by someone inside the ship, or by whoever is holding the ship's remote."

"Maybe Cynthia was injured or something," Demetrius commented. "And perhaps Bradley and Nicola were sent back here on their own."

"So how do we get the stupid thing open?" Claire asked in frustration.

"Hold on," Torin said, going back to his vessel for a pen and paper.

* * *

He knew that whoever was inside the ship could see their surroundings clearly, so he wrote down the instructions for how to locate the correct button, and then held that paper up in front of one of the ship's cameras.

1 Push the top button on the left armrest of the operator's chair.

2 A panel will then pop out.

3 The dark blue button, which is in row 2 on the far right of that panel, opens the door.

Shoop!

As soon as the door opened, Claire ran inside. "Are you okay? What happened?" she asked her friend while hugging her tightly.

Nicola started to cry. "Brad had an accident," she sobbed. "And he didn't get out. Cynthia is in there looking for him. This is so bad…"

* * *

After hugging Demetrius and Torin, and summarizing the details of what happened to Bradley back at Xavier's prison, Torin inquired as to whether or not Nicola had found out what she had been sent to investigate.

"Thankfully, yes," she replied.

Nicola explained exactly what she had seen, and then Torin told her the result of their mission to the lead weather gods' fortress.

"No time to lose, then," Demetrius said. "Nicola, contact Peter immediately."

CHAPTER 31

"Um…" Sophia said to her team while preparing to read the third clue aloud. "I think you better look at this one for yourselves…"

? 3 4 2 1 1

Good luck! We are rooting for you!

Peter couldn't help but shake his head. "I guess even ancient Sevlarians were quirky, eh?" he laughed. "I wonder if this hint was meant to be encouraging, or just sarcastic?"

Zoltan was laughing as well. "Oh, it was written with a positive intention," he told Peter. "Sevlarians are, quite possibly, the least comedic life form in the entire galaxy."

"Speak for yourself," Mr. Winchester smiled. "I think I have turned into quite an entertaining jokester."

Peter looked back and forth at the two

Sevlarians he had so much respect for: Mr. Winchester, his dear mentor, who had spent a huge chunk of his life (even well after he should have retired and moved to a tropical island) ensuring that the innocent people of Earth remained safe. And Zoltan, who with Mr. Winchester's guidance and patience, had finally turned the corner a few years ago and become one of the "good guys."

(Where would Peter's life be today if he hadn't come into contact with these two?)

* * *

"Number puzzles are your forte," Sophia said to her brother.

"I'd say I'm closer to a mezzo-forte," Peter smiled, referencing the *mf* term used to mean *somewhat loud* or *somewhat strong* in sheet music.

"Peter," Mr. Winchester commented. "I think I would pin your ability to solve math problems as fortississimo. That's the one written as *fff,* isn't it?"

Peter and Sophia had a laugh over that comment, as they were once again surprised by the extent to which Mr. Winchester had familiarized himself with things on Earth.

Zoltan, who had no clue what any of them were talking about (and had the "it's all Greek to me" expression on his face), laughed along nonetheless.

* * *

"Assuming that we can ignore the 6 and 8," Mr. Winchester said while thinking aloud. "That leaves us with seven digits left to choose from."

"Perhaps we could start by eliminating any that won't work?" Zoltan suggested. "Which might make finding the correct one a little easier."

Peter grabbed a pen and paper, and wrote down the clue and their list of options.

? 3 4 2 1 1

1
2
3
4
5
~~*6*~~
7
~~*8*~~
9

* * *

It wasn't long before all four were ready to admit that their first approach was not ideal: They couldn't eliminate any digit without knowing what pattern was being used in the number string.

Peter flipped the page over. (He didn't want to crumple it up and drop it, as that would have been a waste of a usable wood product!) He wrote the number string again.

? 3 4 2 1 1

"Pass me that," Sophia said to Peter. "I suck eggs at math, but I just thought of something."

? 3 4 2 1 1

? + 3 = 4   2 = 1 + 1

"I just split up the 6-digit string into two halves," she explained. "Kind of like a mirror, where the equals sign and plus sign are the same distance from the center. What do you think?"

"Well, if you are correct," Zoltan said while weighing the likelihood of this being the solution. "Then we would be shooting for the *1.*"

"May I see that for a second please, Sophia?" Mr. Winchester said politely. "I'd like to explore what happens if we try creating one long equation out of the number string."

? + 3 + 4 − 2 − 1 = 1

"Nope," Mr. Winchester said, laughing a bit. "There's certainly not a 'negative 3 hole' anywhere on the walls..."

"But what if we reversed where you just put the plus and minus signs?" Zoltan suggested. "You know, change the order to minus, minus, plus, plus."

$$? - 3 - 4 + 2 + 1 = 1$$

"Then we'd need a 5 to make the equation mathematically correct," Peter said while looking over Mr. Winchester's shoulder.

Peter needed to investigate things a little further, so he retrieved the paper from Mr. Winchester and wrote down two more options.

$$? + 3 - 4 + 2 - 1 = 1$$

$$? - 3 + 4 - 2 + 1 = 1$$

"Well, isn't that interesting..." Mr. Winchester mentioned once Peter had finished jotting things down. "For both of these new scenarios, a *1* is needed."

"So we now have three reasons to pick *1,*" Sophia said with a smile.

"What's worrying me here," Peter told everyone, "is that if we were to also use times and divided by signs, a whole pile of new possibilities would crop up."

"Hmm..." Mr. Winchester mumbled. "Then

perhaps we need to rethink things." But shortly after, he added another comment. "However, I still like Sophia's original theory, partially because the numbers ascend and then descend."

* * *

Since failing was completely unacceptable, they elected to take a little more time to see what they could come up with. Peter had handed each member a paper and pen, plus he'd written the numbers in the sequence on the top of each one.

* * *

Peter typically liked to pace around while thinking, but the narrowness of their ridge was severely stunting his ability to move around enough to get his brain going. And since he didn't want to accidentally trip and fall into the spikes, he opted for the safest option: sitting cross-legged on the ridge.

This ridge, which had been built who-knows-how-many-hundreds-or-thousands of years ago, was covered in moss, had tons of cracks on it, plus countless ugly weeds growing up through the crevices.

And since Peter's legs were no longer moving (and he needed something to satisfy his urge to fidget), he started yanking at the weeds.

Mr. Winchester and Zoltan were standing together on the far side of the ridge, quietly deliberating some alternatives they thought might have some merit.

* * *

Sophia was mentally exhausted from focusing on this number string for so long, so she went over and sat down beside her brother. She knew from years of watching him that it was best to stay silent for the time being. But after staring at her brother's hand (which was senselessly pulling out weed after weed after weed) she just had to say something.

"Gonna build us a bridge out of those?" she joked.

Peter knew his sister's intentions were good, so he replied in an equally funny and sarcastic way. "I was contemplating it," he joked, "but I doubt it would work…"

Sophia, liking the fact that her brother was smiling again, continued with this silly conversation. "I see," she laughed. "The weeds are too short to build a bridge with, right?"

"Precisely," Peter laughed back. "And unlike the ones that could be pulled out completely in our garden back home, these ones keep breaking off."

(This pointless conversation just kept going and going!)

"Ah…" she said back, almost unable to speak clearly now that she was laughing so hard. "And since the roots stay stuck in the rock, you don't think the weeds are long enough to tie together to make us a bridge?"

Peter's face was beet red as he prepared to reply without bursting into a laughing fit. "Exactly, botanist Sophia," he told his sister. "It's impossible to build a strong bridge without the roots."

Sophia needed a break from this outrageous exchange (so she could catch her breath.) She crawled a few meters away from Peter.

But since their talk of weeds was the freshest thing in her memory, she subconsciously started pulling some out herself, wondering if she could get any of the roots to come out as well.

* * *

Having enjoyed her little break from trying to solve the number string, Sophia was refreshed and ready to get started again.

She took the paper out of her back pocket, unfolded it, and read it again.

? 3 4 2 1 1

Good luck! We are rooting for you!

...

Sophia's eyes then focused on one specific word in the clue. After scanning the numbers twice, she jumped up. "No way!" she cheered. "I think I just figured it out!"

Upon hearing that, Peter also went to jump up, but he (in typical Peter fashion) lost his balance and tripped. (But he was too excited to care how pathetic his tumble had looked.) "What is it? What is it?" he asked.

Sophia had already jotted down some things to make this explanation easier.

? 3 4 2 1 1

? 3
4 2
1 1

"Pete," she said with gusto. "The hint is in the clue! We are rooting for you. ROOTING!"

Peter looked at the notes his sister had written, then up at her face, and back down at the paper again. But he didn't know what she was getting at.

"It's not a 6-digit number sequence," she told her brother. "It's three sets of 2!" She smiled even bigger. "Can't you see how the right number of each set is calculated?" She paused for dramatic effect... "Roots! In each set of 2, the right number is the SQUARE ROOT of the left number! That's why the hint had the word 'root' in it."

Starting from the bottom of Sophia's note, Peter began confirming her theory. "The square root of 1 is 1," he said. "The square root of 4 is 2, and the square root of what is 3?"

Sophia laughed while dancing around.

"9!" Peter cheered, joining in on the dance performance.

Zoltan and Mr. Winchester didn't need to ask the 'Are you sure?' question, as there was absolutely no doubt.

* * *

The 9 was, unfortunately, in a very awkward place as far as aiming was concerned. It was fairly low on the right wall and located way back between the initial ledge and the first ridge.

Zoltan was having an awful time deciding where to stand...

He eventually settled on a spot. "Man, this is going to be hard," he said to himself while trying to steady his arm. "I even need to factor in the parabolic flight path this time."

"Wait!" Peter yelled just before Zoltan's finger got near the trigger.

Zoltan lowered the crossbow and turned around. "You almost gave me a heart attack," he told his friend.

"Did you notice that this time," Peter asked, "the crossbow isn't chained to the pedestal?"

"Oh," Zoltan answered. "Actually, no, I didn't."

"Which means you don't have to stand here to fire it," Peter said next.

"What do you mean?" Sophia asked.

"We can carry it back to the first ridge," Peter explained, "walk up super close to the 9-hole, and shoot it from, like, a meter or so away."

Peter hopped down to the gap between the two ridges. "Carefully pass me the crossbow," he told Zoltan. "Then hop down, go over and climb up on the first ridge, and I'll pass it up to you. Then you can walk over and shot it through the *9* with ease."

* * *

Ninety seconds later, Zoltan was extremely close to the 9-hole, crossbow aimed right at it.

The arrow went into the target, and a few seconds later, the final set of spikes began to lower.

"Sophia!" Mr. Winchester cheered, raising both arms high in the air. "You are as smart, or maybe smarter, than your brother!"

* * *

By the time Zoltan and Peter were back on the second ridge, the spikes were completely gone into the surface below.

Peter and Sophia hopped down first, Zoltan next, then they all helped Mr. Winchester.

Beep-beep-beep-beep.

"That's your communicator, Peter," Zoltan said, pointing at the device in his vest pocket. "The two teams you sent out must have returned from their respective missions."

Peter quickly fumbled for the device. But his hands were sweaty, and before he knew it, it slipped from his grip!

Sophia was watching her clumsy brother and moved like lightning to snatch it before it landed (and smashed) on the rock surface.

"Nice grab," the nervous-looking Peter said.

Sophia returned the communicator to her brother.

Peter looked at the screen, which had nothing more than two very short sentences on it.

You were right! It's a trap!

CHAPTER 32

"Guys!" Peter yelled to his team. "Don't go any further! It's all a set-up! We gotta get out of here! Now!"

The only way to "get out," of course, was to go back through all the areas they had just completed. (And poor Mr. Winchester's ailing knees meant they had to do this painstakingly slowly...)

* * *

"What do you mean it's a trap?" Zoltan asked Peter as they walked out of this big chamber and into the previous one.

"I'll find out the exact details once we get out," Peter replied, speaking quickly because he was so panicked. "But I'm assuming both teams saw what I sent them to look for."

"And what exactly were those missions?" Sophia asked.

"I think I can venture a guess," Mr. Winchester commented. "I suspect that when Torin,

Demetrius, and Claire went to the lead weather gods' meeting chamber—which should have been empty because they are all supposedly trapped in here—they found the lead weather gods were safe and sound inside their fortress, meaning they hadn't been kidnapped at all."

"Ah..." Zoltan nodded. "And what about the team that went to Xavier's prison?"

"Peter likely sent them there," Mr. Winchester continued, "to investigate one simple thing: to see whether or not Argon was being honest with us, or if he was lying and has in fact been working with Xavier on this whole scheme."

"Hold on," Zoltan said. "If Argon was at the prison, that means he has teamed up with Xavier. The other nine lead weather gods don't know this, which means something bad is bound to happen soon!"

* * *

Peter hadn't been timing how long it took them to retrace their steps, but when they finally got back to the entrance of the test site, they had been on the move for at least ten minutes.

All they had to do now was run out the entrance of the caves, jump back on their ships, and get off Sevlar as fast as they could.

But...

But it had taken them too long to get back to

the entrance... They could hear a fierce battle between good and evil weather gods raging just outside the caves.

With no clue as to how many of Xavier's minions were out there battling against Demetrius and Torin, Zoltan realized he had to help immediately. (Thankfully, Zoltan was in possession of the amulet! As long as there weren't too many enemies, he'd be able to blast them away easily.)

Zoltan dashed out and saw right away what was going on: Demetrius and Torin were doing everything they could to prevent Xavier's team—of which there were currently four—from destroying their ships (their only way off the planet!)

Weather gods were not trained to use their powers for battle, but Xavier's men had clearly been practicing that exact thing. They kept shooting powerful wind blasts and lightning bolts toward the ships, which Torin and Demetrius were finding harder and harder to block or deflect.

Since the four evil weather gods were fairly close together, Zoltan started to make a powerful and tight vortex that would lift them off the ground and spin them senseless.

Whack!

But there had been a fifth evil weather god (who had been hiding behind a boulder, specifically watching the cave entrance!)

The blast of wind fired by that hidden evil weather god sent Zoltan flying back hard. He smashed into the rocks next to the cave and dropped to the ground in a heap.

"No!!" Demetrius screamed, running toward his son.

Peter, Sophia, and Mr. Winchester wanted to help, but knew they had to stay in the caves for their own safety.

* * *

"He's still breathing!" Demetrius yelled while checking whether his son was alive or not.

Demetrius then got a look on his face that showed how furious he was at the individual who had just done this to his son. He removed the amulet from Zoltan's pocket, put it in his own cloak, and then sent a massive blast of wind at the evil god who had just knocked Zoltan unconscious.

That evil weather god tried to block Demetrius' attack, but since Demetrius had the amulet, which multiplies one's powers by at least a factor of 100, his efforts were completely useless. He was lifted off his feet and blown over thirty meters backward.

Demetrius should have then refocused his attention on the other four, but rage had affected his usual logical thinking. With the help of the powerful amulet, he prepared another blast of wind to shoot at the same evil weather god.

But nothing happened... Nothing at all!

Xavier's men noticed this mishap, and one of the four quickly took advantage of the opportunity: He smacked Demetrius back with a powerful wind gust.

Demetrius wasn't unconscious, but he was hurt badly. The bone in his left forearm, weakened by his advanced age, had snapped upon impact. He struggled to fight off the brutal pain.

"Stupid old fool!" the one who had just blasted Demetrius laughed. Then he went right back to attacking the ships (which Torin was now defending on his own...)

Now what??

CHAPTER 33

With both Zoltan and Demetrius out of commission, it was only a matter of time before Torin would lose the battle to defend their vessels. (Even though he was both powerful and capable, he was on the wrong side of 5 against 1 odds…)

"Mr. Winchester!" Peter said while pointing up toward what looked to be at least six or seven ships approaching from high above. "Is that Vasilios' team coming to rescue us?"

Mr. Winchester cautiously peered out of the cave and looked up, but then he hung his head. "I'm afraid not, Peter," he said. "Those are part of Xavier's fleet."

"Leonardo!" Demetrius weakly called while holding his bent and broken arm against his stomach. "Please do something! We can't let Xavier get the amulet!"

Too weak to throw it to his friend, he simply rolled it in their direction.

"We have to go and hide this somewhere deep

in the caves," Peter suggested to Mr. Winchester while picking up the amulet. "In a tricky spot where they'll never find it."

"Leonardo, please!" Demetrius called again. "We made a pact over 75 years ago, and I have never broken my promise."

"Pact?" Peter asked Mr. Winchester. "What is he talking about?"

Mr. Winchester had a very conflicted expression on his face. He looked at Peter, and then back at his seriously injured old friend.

"Now keep up your end of the bargain!" Demetrius begged. "You have to do this!"

"Peter, pass me the amulet," Mr. Winchester said, holding his hand out.

Mr. Winchester placed the amulet in his pocket. But instead of disappearing deep into the mountain to go and hide it, he walked out of the caves! He then raised both arms high in the air and started mumbling words that had never come from the mouth of anyone other than a weather god.

(What!? How? Mr. Winchester has... p-p-powers?)

Within seconds, Mr. Winchester was commanding a fierce tornado: one so big and powerful that Peter and Sophia had to grab a nearby tree to prevent themselves from being swallowed by it. His face hardened, and he yelled something that caused the twister to move closer to the five evil weather gods. All five were immediately sucked up into it, and could be seen flailing about while being spun around inside.

Mr. Winchester yelled one more thing. (But whatever he was attempting didn't seem to happen…)

The vortex just kept growing and growing, almost like it was feeding on itself!

Recalling the trouble Zoltan had had with the amulet yesterday, Peter realized the same thing was happening again. He fought the powerful winds while pushing his way over to Mr. Winchester. He reached into the pocket of his elderly friend, removed the amulet (which was pulsating brightly), and took a few steps backward.

The twister began weakening.

Torin used what energy he had left to send that twister out over the sea before Xavier's five escaped from it.

"Peter!" Torin yelled right after that. "Help me carry Zoltan! Nicola, go help Demetrius! Hurry!"

Peter did as he was told, but he was almost in a trance while doing so. (Why had Mr. Winchester been hiding his abilities all this time?)

* * *

They blasted off the surface just in time, and

were headed out of the atmosphere to safety.

(But what about Cynthia and Bradley?)

CHAPTER 34

With Zoltan and Demetrius injured so badly (and Cynthia still on Sevlar), that meant Torin and Mr. Winchester had to pilot the two vessels.

"Are you serious?" Peter said in disbelief after Torin told him that his brother and Cynthia hadn't made it back. "We can't leave them down there! If Xavier finds them, you know he'll torture them!"

Although Torin was also extremely worried about that happening, he attempted to calm Peter down a little. "Cynthia is an amazingly resourceful individual," he told Peter. "Rest assured, she'll find a way to elude Xavier's troops, get to a spot where they can be rescued, and then they'll contact us."

* * *

Since Mr. Winchester was piloting the other ship, Peter was unable to grill him with the countless new questions he now had...

* * *

A few minutes after flying full throttle off Sevlar, they rendezvoused with Vasilios and his fleet.

"All ships, open channel," Mr. Winchester said authoritatively over the microphone.

* * *

Mr. Winchester spent the next ten minutes recounting the specifics of what had happened on Sevlar. (But for some undisclosed reason, he elected to leave out the part about him using his powers to help...)

He finished with a question. "We need to decide what to do about Cynthia and Bradley," he said. "How long do you think we can wait?"

"Leonardo," Vasilios said immediately. "There's no need for ALL of us to wait here. You and Torin should head back to Earth immediately, and get proper medical attention for Zoltan and Demetrius."

"Understood," Torin agreed. "But may I suggest that we switch ships? If Leonardo and I fly the only two undetectable vessels back to Earth, then Xavier's radar will pick you up the instant you enter the atmosphere to rescue Bradley and Cynthia."

"You do have a point," Vasilios replied, "but there would be one significant drawback with that plan: The ships you two are piloting are much, much slower than the ones I and my lead teams are in."

"But isn't being invisible to radar more important than being fast?" Mr. Winchester asked.

"I think speed is all that matters," Vasilios answered. "Because the only way we will know how to find them is when Cynthia pushes her emergency call button. Xavier's team, unfortunately, will pick up that signal as well, meaning they will know exactly where we are headed. It will be a race as to who can get there first."

"Understood," Mr. Winchester replied. "Best of luck to you."

Sophia, crying, walked up and put her mouth up to the microphone without even asking for permission. "Vasilios," she said in a shaky voice. "You have to save Brad, you can't leave him there to die!"

Vasilios picked up on the fear in young Sophia's voice, and he said the only thing he could think of. "My team consists of the elite of the elite," he reassured her. "The instant Cynthia contacts us, we'll swoop in and grab them. I promise."

CHAPTER 35

"It's been over four hours since Leonardo and Torin departed for Earth," Vasilios' second-in-command—who was piloting the ship directly to his right—said into the communicator. "I think we may have to prepare for the worst."

"I agree," another high-ranking member of Vasilios' team added from another ship. "If Cynthia and Bradley haven't been able to get out of the prison by now, then they most likely have already been caught."

"I'm also getting more and more concerned by the minute," Vasilios admitted. "But I still think we need to be patient, just for a little longer. And let's not forget that if we do decide to switch to plan B, a lot of us will not leave this planet alive."

The *Plan B* Vasilios was referring to was more of an all-out attack of the prison facility. (But a haphazard onslaught would be met with force, meaning Xavier's team would battle them to the death.)

* * *

After another two hours of waiting, Vasilios made an announcement. "Starting now," he told the captains of the other ships, "I want fifty percent of each crew to sleep for the next four and a half hours: Three 90-minute sleep cycles should be enough to feel rested."

This may have sounded more like a suggestion than an order, but all captains immediately put it into action.

(They all wanted to know how much longer they would wait until going to Plan B, but no one was brave enough to ask...)

CHAPTER 36

Zoltan and his father were now at Stoneburg Memorial Hospital being treated for their respective injuries.

The break in Demetrius' arm was a bad one, but thankfully the bone hadn't pierced the skin, and the break itself was fairly clean. It would just need to be put into a cast to allow for healing. The doctors wanted to let the swelling settle for another day or two before repositioning it and wrapping up his arm.

Zoltan was much worse off than his father, though. The head knock, which the doctors were worried might have been strong enough to cause bleeding in the brain, was fortunately just a concussion. But he had also broken four ribs when his back impacted against the rock. Three out of the four were hair-line fractures, but the fourth one was quite nasty. They were unsure whether or not it had punctured his lung, so they were keeping him in the ICU and monitoring him very carefully for the time being.

CHAPTER 37

"Vasilios! Wake up!" the crew member who was in charge while Vasilios slept said while shaking him awake. "Cynthia has just turned on her locater beacon!"

Even though he had been sound asleep ten seconds earlier, Vasilios dashed to the pilot seat like he was a 100-meter sprint finalist.

"Onyx! Klaron!" he said loudly into the microphone. "We are going in, now! Follow me!"

The captains of both ships replied, "Yes, sir," and the three ships shot toward Sevlar's surface.

* * *

"We're almost there," Vasilios announced while rocketing closer and closer to the position the homing device was directing them to. "We should be able to land in a minute or two."

"Bad news, boss," Onyx said. "Looks like we've got company."

"Really?" Vasilios reacted with surprise. "I don't see any ships anywhere."

"They're not coming by air," Onyx explained, being more precise. "They're heading toward Cynthia's location in some sort of land vehicles, possible armored trucks?"

"Oh, I see them now," Vasilios replied. "Looks like there are four trucks in total. This is going to be difficult... Very difficult."

"I can see Cynthia and Bradley!" Onyx yelled into his microphone when they were about a hundred meters from their landing spot. They are hiding behind that rock."

* * *

The location Cynthia and Bradley had managed to get to was a good three kilometers from the prison entrance. She had likely chosen this spot to give Vasilios' team enough time to get to them before Xavier's troops did.

Cynthia sent a blast of wind at the lead truck, hoping to flip it over. It wasn't enough to knock it on its side, but she did manage to twist it, which forced the other trucks to temporarily stop.

* * *

Xavier's men jumped from their vehicles at the same instant Vasilios' team exited their ships. And the battle ensued immediately.

Since Vasilios' crew had prepared extensively for this, each person in the 12-member team knew their responsibility: six were tasked with defending their ships, four were to attack Xavier's men, and two needed to provide cover so that Cynthia and Bradley could run over safely.

Vasilios' group was strong, but Xavier's team was equally capable and powerful. The battle of wind and lightning was fierce. Although there were no injuries yet, it was only a matter of time before something happened...

* * *

They managed to provide enough "cover" to allow Cynthia and Bradley to sprint over without being harmed. Cynthia knew she needed to help, so she ordered Bradley into Vasilios' ship while she joined the fight.

"More trucks approaching!" Klaron yelled. "We'll never be able to hold them all off!"

"Then we need to depart right now!" Onyx yelled.

"But they'll destroy the ships the instant we board them!" Cynthia screamed.

"Everyone!" Vasilios announced, acting quickly. "On the count of three, send the strongest wind blast you can muster. If we all do this at the same time, we should be able to knock them far enough away to give us time to escape. One, two, three!"

Vasilios' scheme was more or less successful. When the thirteen of them combined their wind blasts into one powerful stream, it overwhelmed Xavier's team and sent them flying far back.

"Onto the ships!" Vasilios yelled. "Hurry!"

* * *

With the doors of the other two ships now shut,

Vasilios stood at the entrance of his. (But he didn't like what he saw…)

Xavier's reinforcements were racing over to join the fight, and they were getting very close. Plus, Xavier's original ten attackers were almost ready to start battling again. (Even if Vasilios' ships launched within the next ten seconds or so, Xavier's men would easily knock them from the sky.)

Vasilios made a split-second decision: he jumped out of his ship, shouted the "Shut door" command, and pushed the communicator on his shoulder. "All ships! Depart now! Go!" he yelled.

"But what about—" Onyx started to ask, right before Vasilios cut the connection.

The launching of a ship was a 2-part process: First, a ship used special thrusters to lift itself ten or fifteen meters off the ground, and from there, it began accelerating.

Vasilios' eyes kept flipping back and forth between the three ships and Xavier's approaching men.

* * *

As soon as all three ships were no longer touching Sevlar's surface, Vasilios used every bit of power he had left to shake the ground as hard as he could.

The massive earthquake had the desired effect. It caused everyone on Xavier's team to fall down (and temporarily stay down), meaning they couldn't create any wind to knock the ships out of the sky.

When the evil weather gods regained their balance, all three ships were high above, far out of Xavier's team's reach.

Vasilios, of course, realized he had no chance against Xavier's group now. He guessed they wouldn't kill him yet, as Xavier would want to interrogate him first.

But for some reason, Vasilios felt at peace with himself. He knew how old he was, and he knew he had finally fulfilled his promise to help Sevlar in its darkest days. He had lived a long life, and could feel satisfaction in knowing it hadn't been for nothing.

He wouldn't be around to see if Xavier could finally be defeated, but knowing that such a thing might now happen brought a smile to his face.

He turned around and clasped his arms behind his back. (A weather god could not use his powers without moving his arms.) Vasilios had just surrendered.

Klaron's vessel was equipped with a powerful camera, one that allowed him a clear view of Vasilios, even from so high up. "Vasilios has surrendered," he announced into his communicator. "He—" Klaron gulped.

"Klaron!?" Onyx said. "What just happened?"

"One of Xavier's men ignored the fact that Vasilios had surrendered," he replied angrily.

"And hit him with a huge lightning blast. He's face-first on the ground now."

"Is he dead?" Onyx asked.

"Probably, but I can't be sure," Klaron replied. "That lightning blast short-circuited the heartrate monitor, so we have no way of checking his vital signs anymore."

Since Vasilios had sacrificed himself, the successful rescue of Cynthia and Bradley had been very anti-climactic.

CHAPTER 38

Vasilios was survived by three children, seven grandchildren, and two great-grandchildren. (His wife had passed away six years ago, mere weeks after the birth of their first great-granddaughter.)

Sevlar was very unlike Earth when it came to the custom of funerals: funeral proceedings were more similar to "celebrations."

* * *

A week after their return to Earth, they booked the big banquet hall at the hotel for an event to pay respect to Vasilios. It seemed almost like a giant party: food, dancing, a magic show for the kids, tons of silly games and contests. There was only one short speech, which was given by his eldest child. (And as was custom on Sevlar, no tears were shed, and the speech was very humorous.)

Peter had set up a camera and was currently broadcasting the evening's proceedings to the TV in Zoltan's hospital room.

By the end of his speech, every single guest was red-faced from laughing. (This was considered the most respectful way to send someone off: by letting him or her know how much joy they brought to others.)

* * *

"Peter," Mr. Winchester said to him when all the younger kids were doing a relay race. "May I speak to you outside for a minute? I believe I have some explaining to do."

"I guess," Peter reacted coolly... (But then he decided to hear Mr. Winchester out before judging him.) "Sure, let's go."

* * *

"When I was ten years old," Mr. Winchester began, "I went to visit Demetrius' family in his small hometown during a festival one summer. Demetrius and I were always getting into trouble, but only about silly little things.

"During the afternoon of the festival's highlight—when we should have been at the event enjoying the fun and games—we hiked up into one of the nearby mountains. We were at the age where we would soon discover whether or not we had any powers, and both of us desperately wanted to know.

"Demetrius went first. He had memorized the phrase which was supposed to conjure up a thunderstorm. He concentrated hard, and managed to make a couple of small cumulonimbus clouds accumulate near our location. Sounds like a failure, but for a young kid to be able to do that is very impressive.

"Then I went next. I had written down the phrase for causing earthquakes. I recited it in my head a few times, and then I tried using it to see if anything would happen.

"Unlike Demetrius' *tiny* success, the earthquake I created was surprisingly big. As soon as I realized what I had done, I stopped, but it was already too late.

"You see, part of his hometown was on the side of a mountain, and my earthquake triggered a landslide, which completely destroyed seven homes."

"Oh my," Peter said in shock. "How many people died?"

"Thankfully, none," Mr. Winchester replied. "There weren't any injuries either. The annual festival is held near the river on the opposite side of town, and always attended by everyone who lives there.

"And that's when Demetrius and I made that pact: He promised to never tell anyone that the earthquake hadn't been a natural one. And in return, I promised to never use my powers again, unless he instructed me to."

"But you were just a kid," Peter said. "If you had come clean, they would have understood, and probably would have forgiven you."

"They might have forgiven me," Mr. Winchester continued, "but Demetrius and I would have received the standard punishment for anyone who attempts to test their abilities before the age of thirteen. And that punishment is a lifetime ban from ever being allowed to use those powers again. Demetrius was set on becoming a weather god when he grew up, so me admitting my mistake—and the fact that he was with me when I did it—would have meant the same punishment for the both of us. He would have been deprived of his dream."

"But how did you become so good at using your powers?" Peter asked. "From what I saw back on Sevlar, you certainly aren't a beginner."

"Since I taught at the training academy for so long," Mr. Winchester answered, "I had easy access to all the materials at the school. I studied in private for over a decade. And I also practiced, in far-off locations, on holidays."

Peter finally smiled a little. "And kept up that study and practice on Earth too, right?" he asked.

"Oh, yes," Mr. Winchester answered. "Not only that, but I also helped out when and where I could. You know, I helped stop disasters that Zoltan refused to help with. Well, ones that he wouldn't notice me helping with. But I should also add this: when I used the amulet on Sevlar last week, something went wrong. Even with the amulet's help, I never should have been able to make that large of a tornado."

Peter looked into the eyes of his dear friend: the poor old man looked so conflicted. But Peter knew Mr. Winchester's caring heart had never waned.

"Ah, this massively powerful precious stone..." Peter said while reaching into his pocket and removing the amulet (which he had been holding onto for *safekeeping* since returning from Sevlar.) Without even flinching, he passed it to Mr. Winchester. "As my therapist has told me numerous times," Peter said, high-fiving his elderly friend, "there's no sense in dwelling on the past. Plus, I see your powers as a big advantage for us. It'll certainly increase our chances of taking down Xavier once and for all."

"Thank you, Peter," Mr. Winchester smiled, eyes wet with tears. "Hearing that from you means a lot to me."

"I do have a favor to ask, though," Peter said next. "Think you can teach me some of those tricks? I mean, I'd love to be able to command the weather a little."

Mr. Winchester burst out laughing. "I only wish," he grinned. "Unfortunately, only those with Sevlarian DNA are capable of that."

"Shucks," Peter laughed. "Well, then I guess I'll just have to live vicariously through you."

"Vicariously?" Mr. Winchester replied. "What's that mean?"

"Check your dictionary," Peter smiled.

Thank you for reading *Outrageously Puzzled.* I really hope you enjoyed the latest part of Peter's puzzle-filled adventure! And I would be super appreciative if you kindly took a quick minute to review it on Amazon or Goodreads. Thank you so much!

There is still a lot of excitement (and puzzles, of course!) to come for Peter and his friends! I'll try my very best to get Book 8 done by October 2022!

And if you have any questions (or comments/advice/suggestions) please feel free to contact me (pj@pjnichols.com). Each and every message I receive makes my day, and the wonderful suggestions and ideas (from readers all over the globe) have been awesomely helpful!

Sincerely,

P.J. Nichols

Milton Keynes UK
Ingram Content Group UK Ltd.
UKHW030759101224
3488UKWH00001B/14